TRAPPED BY LIES

TRUTH OR LIES BOOK 3

ELLA MILES

FREE BOOKS

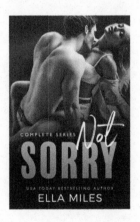

Read **Not Sorry** for **FREE**! And sign up to get my latest releases, updates, and more goodies here→EllaMiles.com/freebooks

Follow me on BookBub to get notified of my new releases and recommendations here→Follow on BookBub Here

Join Ella's Bellas FB group to grab my **FREE** book **Pretend I'm Yours**→Join Ella's Bellas Here

TRUTH OR LIES SERIES

1

KAI

MY HEART HEALED—WHOLLY and completely. I forgave the man I thought had sold me. I did the impossible. I was wrong about Enzo. He didn't sell me. He's not responsible for all of the hurt I endured for six years.

My father is responsible.

My heart healed, only to break a second later.

Enzo didn't sell me before, but he did now.

He sold me to Milo Wallace.

Milo—a man I only spent twenty-four hours with and already my body became as scared, broken, and bruised as the entire first month I spent with Jarod. Milo has taken women before, that much is clear. He's practiced in breaking people slowly and methodically. I still don't understand how I got out of there without him raping me. Unless, this was his plan the entire time. To let me think I was free, only to buy me back and force me to do whatever he wants.

And I know if Milo gets me back, this time my body won't be off limits to him. This time I won't be able to buy my freedom by enduring beatings or giving him a precious ring. This time, Milo will ruin me.

Milo's coming in an hour, and I'm not sure I can stop him.

Enzo's words cut through the fog.

I blink rapidly, trying to bring myself back to the real world. I'm standing in the bedroom I've shared with Enzo since he took me as his captive. I've spent all this time wishing he would set me free, wishing for a way out, but now I'd do anything to continue to be Enzo's prisoner. I know what Enzo expects of me. And he'd never force me to do anything I didn't want to do. Enzo would never hurt me, not like Milo would.

Sold.

I never thought I would be sold again. Never thought I'd be stupid enough to let it happen. But being sold isn't about being naive. It's completely out of my control.

I could fight.

I could run.

But I won't be able to do either without Enzo agreeing. I can't fight two armies of men.

One hour.

That's how much time I have.

One fucking hour left of freedom, if you can even call my current situation free.

I should be talking to Enzo about what he's going to do to try to keep from letting me go. Or what his plan is to get me back if he does have to give me to Milo.

But I can't.

My heart hurts too much.

Enzo betrayed me, even after I did everything to try and protect him.

It fucking hurts.

I feel a tear well up, but I won't let it fall. Enzo doesn't get to see my pain. And neither does Milo when he arrives.

I'm numb—that's where I'll go. My body has prepared time and time again for this exact situation. I'm not even scared anymore. My body will lockdown for as long as I need to survive.

Enzo says something to me, but I don't hear it. I've already locked him out. He doesn't get to see inside my mind. He lost the right to talk to me, to touch me, to be anything other than my enemy.

His mouth moves again, but my ears have learned to filter out the sound.

The door opens, and Langston and Zeke enter.

My heart starts to open again at the sight of the two men —men I consider friends.

No, close it. Don't open it. They work for Enzo—not me. They will hurt me the same as Enzo. And when the time comes, they will turn me over to Milo with one word from Enzo. They won't try to stop it, no matter how much they want to save me—they won't.

I watch the exchange between the three men, like I'm in a tank at the aquarium filled with water and they are on the other side of the glass. I can see them, I know they are there, but I can't hear them.

Enzo paces frantically in the bedroom. Langston reaches out to touch him, but Enzo swats his arm down.

I think they are yelling, arguing, but I can't imagine what about. Enzo sold me. The deal is done. Enzo Black is a man of his word. He can't back out of the deal now. It would ruin him and Black's reputation. He would never put me above the Black empire. And I wouldn't want him to. Other people shouldn't suffer because of me. I just wish Enzo would have trusted me enough to know I would never willingly betray him. I would never hurt him if I could avoid it.

Never.

Apparently, Enzo didn't feel the same way.

The sound of the doorbell downstairs alerts my senses. It's the first sound I've heard in over an hour.

An hour—has it really been that long?

The bedroom door opens, and Westcott pokes his head in.

Enzo gives Westcott an order, and I'm sure he's going to greet Milo Wallace. My time is almost up.

What will happen to the Black empire with me gone? Will Archard call for the next game, and when I don't show up, will Enzo win by default?

It's better this way. I may have won the first round, but I don't want an evil empire. Not even to try and turn it good. I want nothing to do with this life anymore.

Enzo walks over to me and puts his hands on my shoulders, squeezing tightly. It should burn, the fire in him should light up every nerve in my body like he has countless times before. But I feel nothing. He might as well not be touching me.

He opens his mouth, but again I don't hear him.

I've shut him out. The pain is too much.

"Kai! Listen to me!" Enzo's voice booms, somehow cutting through the brick wall I put up to lock him out.

I blink, the only indication that I heard him.

"I have a plan—trust me. I will never let any man hurt you," Enzo says.

His words mean nothing.

"Kai?" Enzo asks hesitantly, trying to see if I heard him or not.

I snap my head to him; my eyes blacken into slits, shooting all my anger at him. But I don't say anything.

He sighs with a whimper of agony and fear filling the room with his despair.

Good, he deserves to be in as much pain and anguish as I am. I want to hurt him as badly as I can before I leave.

"I will never let another man hurt you. Truth or lie?" he asks.

He waits.

I wait.

The pause stretches.

I want his words to be truth so badly. I want to feel hope.

For him.

For us.

For myself.

But my heart knows the truth—I can't trust Enzo Black.

"Lie," I answer.

His face falls into darkness like I plunged a blade into his heart.

Enzo drops his hands from my shoulders, and then he looks at Zeke and motions for him to stay with me. To watch guard over me and make sure I don't do something stupid like try to leave or kill myself to avoid being sold to Milo.

Enzo wipes the moisture from his eyes and then transforms into the fiercest demon I've ever seen. No one would ever know Enzo's heart was breaking just a moment ago. He's one determined motherfucker. He's just not my black knight, my savior.

He sold me.

The truth rings in my head as I watch Langston and Enzo leave.

Enzo sold me, and he doesn't know if he can stop it.

2

ENZO

KAI'S WORDS WRECK ME.

I deserve them though. I have to earn her trust again. I have to protect her at all costs.

Even at the cost of the Black empire. I would give it all to Milo today if I thought that would keep her safe.

It won't.

For one, it would only make Milo realize how much I care about Kai. It would make him want her more—hurt her more.

No, sacrificing my men and empire to Milo wouldn't save Kai.

I have to find a way to keep Kai and my men safe. *But how?*

I told Kai I have a plan—I don't.

I could offer myself up in exchange for her. But that would leave Kai vulnerable with no one left to protect her. And Milo has no use for me; he'd just kill me or sell me to my enemies. I'm not a good exchange for Kai. He knows someone else would take my place, and he still wouldn't have what he wants—Kai.

Milo Wallace is a wealthy and dangerous man. He doesn't have as large of an empire as I do, but it's impressive all the same. He won't go down easily. And it's going to be hard for me to back out of the deal I struck with him. That's not who Black is. Black doesn't back down from a deal.

How could I have been so stupid and reckless? Because I was raised by the devil. And no matter how hard I try to fight off that side of myself, it always creeps back in when I lose self-control—when I let the anger in.

Kai deserves so much better. When I find a way to save her, I have to let her go before I hurt her again and again. I have to win to keep her out of this life. I have to protect her always. And getting her as far away from the monster within me is the best way to do that.

Langston and I walk toward my office where I told West-cott to bring Milo. He trades me a nervous glance as we approach. Langston has had faith in my leadership abilities time and time again. He knows I'm capable of leading my men to safety. I will do whatever it takes to keep everyone safe. But Langston, Zeke, and I talked for the entire hour, and I couldn't come up with a plan to save Kai.

The only solution I've come up with is to kill the bastard sitting in my office. But it would ignite a war—one the Black empire couldn't handle fighting at the moment. Not when Kai and I would have to agree before we made any move.

But I'll start the war if that is the only way to keep Kai safe.

I reach the closed door to my office. "Stay here," I say to Langston.

He nods solemnly, and it's the first time I don't feel complete faith from Langston in my abilities.

Zeke already swore he'd take Kai and run off if it came

down to it to protect her. Langston feels pretty much the same.

It's the first time I think they would disobey my orders if I told them to turn her over to Milo. And it's the first time I'm thankful for their rebelliousness.

But I can't let them run away with Kai. Milo would hunt them down and kill them all.

There has to be another way.

I let the fire grow, burn, and ignite until the monster within is focused on saving Kai and on protecting my men.

I'm not a superhero.

I'm not a savior.

I'm not a good man.

And right now, no one believes I can or will protect Kai without hurting those who work for me—but I will find a way.

My father may have turned my soul into the devil—the kind to turn on Kai the second I thought she turned on me. But it's also the ruthless kind to destroy anyone in my path. And right now I'm set on saving Kai.

I promised to never let another man hurt her—and that includes me.

I open the door and step into the office like the fucking king I am. Milo Wallace will not know my anger. He will not know my fury or rage. And he most definitely will not see my fear.

Milo will be clueless to my intentions. He will never know offering to sell Kai to him was the worst mistake of my life. When I picked up the phone to call him, I thought this is what she wanted. Maybe not to be sold, but to be with a man she chose. I was idiotic for thinking that. And Kai doesn't deserve to be sold—ever.

"Mr. Wallace, it's a pleasure to see you again," I say, holding out my hand to him.

He grins evilly as he shakes my hand, trying to look into the depths of my eyes to get a glimpse of my feelings. He doesn't have a clue though.

"Please, call me Milo, Mr. Black," Milo says.

I don't offer for him to call me Enzo—not in my office. Not when he's taking what's *mine*. I am Mr. Black here. I am power itself, and by the time this meeting is over, I will have a plan.

"Take a seat," I say, as I take a seat behind my desk. Westcott already has a scotch sitting at my desk, and Milo has one in his left hand.

"How's business going?" I ask.

"Good. You?"

"Good." Neither of us gives anything away. We both know better than to let anything slip out the other could use as leverage.

"Five million is a lot of money for a whore," Milo says.

Do. Not. React.

I force the calm stillness to take over. I kick back in my chair as I nurse my scotch.

"Five million is nothing to men like us."

He gives me a slight nod.

"Still, I usually don't go higher than one million."

"I won't accept anything less than five. One million isn't even worth my time for this meeting." *Is this the way? Can it truly be this easy?* He won't pay more than one million for Kai. I can refuse to sell her because I want more money.

Milo smirks and then reaches into his pocket and pulls out a ring.

A ring I recognize immediately—*my mother's ring.*

The ring Kai gave to Milo so he wouldn't rape her. A

ring I owe everything to for saving Kai, yet also want to curse for making me believe Kai betrayed me.

Milo cocks his head. "This looks like an engagement ring to me, Black."

I nod nonchalantly. "It is."

He twirls the ring around his pinky finger. "Why would you sell the whore you married?"

I laugh like it's the most ridiculous thing. "You think I married the bitch?" I hate myself for calling Kai a bitch, but he needs to think she means nothing to me.

"Yes."

I shake my head. "I didn't marry her."

"Then why did you give her this ring?"

"So the world would know she's mine."

He leans back studying me, but I pour all my truth into my words. Those words at least are true. Kai is mine, and I wanted the world to know.

"The scars and bruises weren't enough?" Milo tests me. He doesn't believe I was the one who marked her.

"You know how men are. I beat her black and blue plenty of times, but that wasn't enough to stop other men from touching her. Only that ring did that."

"She didn't look too beat up at my party."

"I've grown bored with her lately. I've had her for six years. She earned a night of freedom, and when I saw your infatuation with her, I realized I had found a buyer willing to pay top price."

"She means nothing to you?"

"Nothing."

He sighs. "Then she isn't worth five million."

I shrug. "Probably not. I broke her easily. You got a taste of her on your yacht, which for that alone I should double the price. You didn't have any right to touch what was mine without paying."

I lean forward, threatening Milo with everything in my body. "I think I will raise the price—ten million. You saw something in her on your yacht. You want her; you pay for her. And you pay for your mistake touching her."

Milo's eyes light up. *Fuck. I fucked up.* He realizes what she means to me. He pockets the ring again.

His phone buzzes. He glances down, and his pupils dilate. He doesn't answer the phone. He silences it only for it to start buzzing again. And that's when I realize *his mistake*. He has enemies here. Someone he's running from.

"When do you leave?" I ask.

"Tonight." He answers, but his thoughts aren't on this conversation. They are on the buzzing in his pocket. "I should be going. Arrangements need to be made for my departure."

"Back to Italy?"

He doesn't answer. He doesn't want me to know where he's going. He wants to hurt me. He wants Kai. But he doesn't feel safe here in Miami. With one phone call I'll find out who his greatest enemy in town is, and then I'll use it to my advantage.

I will keep Kai safe.

"Do we have a deal?" I ask, holding out my hand already knowing he's going to take it. He risked his empire all to claim my woman. He wants to hurt me; I just wish I knew why. At his party he acted like we were great friends. But that's how enemies behave in public, like the best of friends. Only in private do we dare to make moves against each other.

He grips it and then pulls out his phone. He speaks to his right-hand man, and I know the money is in my account.

I don't verify it. I don't give a shit about the money. That's not what this is about.

Milo wants power over me, and he's taking it. He set a trap to get me to sell Kai, and I fell for it. He won this round, just as Kai won her first round in our game. But I never lose twice against the same opponent. The next round goes to me, and I will slaughter him.

"The whore?" Milo asks, watching my reaction when he calls Kai a whore again.

"Westcott," I say.

The door opens, and Westcott steps inside. "Have Langston bring me Miss Miller."

"Yes, Mr. Black," Westcott answers.

I want to add—slowly. Take your fucking time so I can make Milo squirm. The second he gets back I know he will depart. I only have minutes to make my plan work, but I don't doubt I can make it happen. I can save Kai while keeping up the ruse that I want to sell her.

I take out my cell phone. "I just need to confirm you made the payment, and then the whore is yours."

I dial Zeke's number.

"Do you have a fucking plan?" Zeke answers.

"Yes, I'd like to confirm Milo Wallace deposited ten million into my account," I say, even though I don't give a shit if the money was deposited, and I know Zeke won't either.

"Shit, Langston said he's here to take her to Milo. You better have a fucking plan Enzo, or I'll kill you myself. We don't sell women. We fight, we kill to protect our empire, but we never sell women like objects." He pauses. "I'm letting her go, but you better have a fucking plan."

"How much longer until you find out if the money is there? Mr. Wallace is in a hurry," I say, trying to let Zeke know he doesn't have much time to do what I want him to do.

Zeke sighs into the phone. "I'll find out everything I can about Milo. But we already know everything. We know his organization. His number two. His allies. And his enemies."

"Yes, can you read that last number again?"

"His enemies? I should focus on his enemies?"

"Yes, thank you for confirming the deposit." I end the call, knowing I gave Zeke all the information to get started searching for Milo's enemy. The one closest to Miami. The biggest threat.

"The money has been confirmed," I say to Milo.

"Good. Now, where's my whore?"

"She's coming. One of my men is bringing her now."

There is a knock, and my heart stops.

I hate this plan.

I would much rather shoot Milo here now, but that could put Kai at bigger risk. Men would know she's my weakness. They would try to take her just to control me.

Langston opens the door and escorts Kai in, holding onto her bicep. Kai doesn't look at me, nor Milo. She's a stone fortress blocking everything out. She doesn't even react to Langston's touch on her arm.

Milo looks her up and down. "Good. Sorry for cutting this short, but I really should be going."

I nod. "Of course, we won't keep you waiting."

I'm heartless. I beg my heart to stop beating because I know this is going to rip it to shreds.

Milo stands up and grabs Kai by the wrist.

She doesn't flinch.

God, she's so fucking strong.

This ends here. This is the last time a man touches her without her permission. I don't care how many times she betrays me; I won't hurt her or let anyone else hurt her again.

I want to tell Kai this with my eyes and soul. I want her to believe me, but she won't—not until I prove it over and over and over.

I nod to Langston, and he releases his grip on her arm. Milo starts leading her out the door, pulling her too forcibly. But I compel my body to stay in my seat until he's gone.

I will get her back. She will not take a step onto that yacht. Even if I have to shoot Milo myself and start an impossible war. I will not let her get hurt.

Kai's eyes fall to mine, surprising the hell out of me.

I promise her with my eyes. "I will save you—trust me," I mouth.

"I know," she mouths back, and then she's gone.

I'm gutted.

How can she put faith in me after everything I did? After I'm letting a man, who has beaten her before, take her? Did something happen up in that bedroom while I was gone? Did Zeke say something? How can she trust me?

Because I'm her only hope. She has no choice but to put her faith in me.

I can still earn her forgiveness, not that I deserve it. I don't want to be redeemed. I only want to keep her safe.

I hear the front door shut from my office where Langston stands looking at me like he's ready to kill me. But I don't have time to explain myself to him. There is work to do. And I will not fail.

I close my eyes letting the pain I deserve in, because watching another man take Kai was the hardest fucking thing I've ever done.

3

KAI

EACH STEP away from Enzo's office physically hurts.

Each fucking step is another memory of his betrayal. Of the pain he caused me. He fucked up, and somehow I'm the one paying for his mistakes.

Stop.

I can't think about what Enzo did that landed me in this mess. I can't think about what my father did that started this all. I can't think about anything other than finding a way out.

I will never be someone's slave. *Never again.*

I'd rather die.

Have faith in Enzo—trust him. Enzo's done everything he can to protect me, and even though he's the reason Milo is taking me, he's the best hope I have at getting free.

But didn't I learn from last time I can't have hope in anyone coming to rescue me?

Enzo didn't know I was taken, last time though. He didn't make me a promise to keep me safe. To prevent any other man from harming me ever again.

I can't rely on my father or anyone else coming to save me, but maybe I can count on Enzo coming.

Milo leads me to a blacked out SUV. He opens the door and releases my wrist, waiting for me to get into the car, but not controlling me. He wants me to surrender to him —*never going to happen.*

"Get in the car, Mrs. Black," Milo says.

I narrow my eyes and scowl. I know Enzo didn't confirm our marriage. That would look like a weakness if he gave up his wife to a man like Milo.

"It's Miller, Kai Miller," I snap.

"No, it's not. It's Black. I don't buy Enzo's bullshit. You mean something to him. He gave you his mother's ring. But I don't know why he sold you. Oh well, his loss is my gain." Milo sweeps my hair off my neck.

I jump at his touch. Not because his fingers swept over a bruise, but because Milo is the last man on this earth I want touching me.

He grins at my reaction. "You're jumpier than the last time we met. Is there a reason for it?"

I growl. "You're a monster."

"No." He leans down until his breath is at my ear. "I'm your new master."

I shiver.

"And if you don't get in the car right now, I'll beat you until our previous meeting doesn't even register on your pain scale anymore," he says.

I glance behind me to the door of the beach house I've come to feel like home.

It's not my home. It betrayed me.

And even though the only people who give the tiniest of shits if I live or die are all inside its walls, none come for me. None fight for me. I'm on my own.

I take a deep breath, knowing I have to choose my battles if I'm going to survive. And refusing to get into the car won't help me. Not when Enzo will order Langston or Zeke to put me in the car themselves if I try to run.

I climb into the car, all the way to the far side, and then Milo slides into the seat next to me. Two men sit in the front seat. Neither of them speak or turn to look at us; they remain focused on the windshield as if they are statues.

But Milo nods, and the car starts driving forward. As soon as we exit Enzo's property, we are surrounded by half a dozen more cars that feel more like tanks than ordinary vehicles. All driving around us, like Milo is the fucking president or something.

"Is the protection really necessary? Enzo sold me; I don't think he will be rushing to try and get me back," I snap.

"Enzo isn't my enemy—at least he isn't today. I have many enemies in this country. But don't worry, I have the best team; I won't let anyone hurt you but me."

I want to fight—that's my initial reaction. It's been a long time since I truly got to fight.

With Jarod, I learned to lock my mind and heart away. I blocked it all out after the first few months.

But I'm tired of blocking it all out. I won't let my mind shut down and put up walls anymore. I'm still just as fucked up after shutting it all out. It didn't truly protect me. *Maybe if I had continued to fight day after day, I wouldn't be so fucked up now?*

So that's my plan. To never stop fighting. To fight until I have nothing left. To fight until Enzo saves me or I die.

Enzo Black may be a monster. The kind of man who would sell me because of my disloyalty. But that is only half of who Enzo is. The other half protects the innocent and deserving. He will do everything he can to protect me. Even if it takes him years, he will come for me. And I won't lock away what's left of me while I wait. I won't go backward. Enzo helped me heal, and although I have a long way yet to go, I won't let Milo break any of my progress.

When Enzo saves me, I will remain as I am. Not because Enzo deserves to have me whole, but because I do. I deserve to stay healed. I deserve to remain strong. I deserve to remain Kai Miller.

"I can't wait to get you alone," Milo says, reaching over and stroking my arm with his finger.

Fight.

I grab his finger and twist as hard as I can, hoping to break it, and if not, do some amount of damage.

He doesn't make a sound. Not one moan of agony. He removes his hand seamlessly from my grasp.

"You're a fighter, I'll give you that. I wasn't sure after our previous encounter where you just locked that pretty little mind away. This version of you will be so much more enjoyable."

He slaps me across the cheek. I feel the burn of his touch. I feel the sting as our skin collides. My head whips to the side, but I feel nothing beneath the outer layer of my skin.

No fear.

No pain.

Nothing.

I study myself, trying to determine if I locked my soul inside again to protect myself.

I didn't. I'm still here. But my fury is bigger than the pain. My determination at fighting is stronger.

"Tell me about Enzo. Tell me how you two met," Milo says.

I open my mouth to refuse when Milo's phone rings. I

hear the buzzing in his pocket, and I look out the window at the passing palm trees.

Milo speaks into the phone, but I don't listen. I try to enjoy the sunlight pouring in. I don't know the next time I'll feel the warmth from the sun on my skin.

He ends the call. "It's time for us to have a chat."

I turn my attention back to him, just as his phone buzzes again. He growls as he looks at the number and decides to answer it. "Yes," he hisses into the phone.

I watch as Milo gets four more phone calls. All from numbers he chooses to answer. Each call lasts five minutes or longer. Each call distracts and irritates Milo further. But he answers them. Each and every one.

Enzo.

Is he arranging these calls? Finding a way to distract Milo to protect me?

Yes, I feel it.

But how long can he keep this up? And once we get to wherever Milo is taking me, then what? Enzo can't keep having the entire city call Milo.

I need to fight.

I don't know if Enzo is going to be able to get me back for a long time, but I can try now—while Milo is distracted.

I need a weapon.

I can't overpower Milo. The door is locked, and there is no way to unlock it from the back seat so I can't run. The only chance I have is to find a weapon.

I'm sure Milo has a gun on him. Enzo, Langston, and Zeke all carry a weapon near their waist. But I don't see anything visible on Milo from where I'm sitting.

I glance down to his thick boots. Enzo also carries knives in his boots.

I'd rather have a gun. Langston and Zeke taught me how

to shoot. If I had a gun, I'd kill Milo. Although, Milo's two goons in the front would probably shoot me before I had a chance to turn the gun on them. It would be worth it to know Milo is dead. His men might finish me off, but not before I destroyed Milo.

But if he's carrying a knife near his ankle, that would be easier for me to get than a gun in a waistband buried beneath his jacket.

Milo's eyes are trained out the window as he barks into the phone. Something about having plenty of fuel by the time we get there, or he'll kill them all.

Fuel?

I look out the front window, and that's when I realize where we are going—his yacht.

Fuck.

I will not get on his yacht. I can't. I'd rather die.

Seeing the dock and his yacht looming in the distance fans my desire to act. I must act—now.

I glance over at Milo one more time, trying to decide where I'm most likely to find a weapon. And one I can easily retrieve. I decide to go for the ankle.

I bend down, pretending to mess with my own shoe. My eyes focus down, trying not to draw any attention from the three men in the car. When Milo's voice grows loud again, I make my move.

I slip my hand under his pant's leg until I feel metal. Then, I grab it—my body launching over Milo's as the knife lands at his throat.

The car lurches trying to throw me off Milo, but I hold the knife steady to his throat, watching as he swallows carefully.

He laughs and ends the call without a goodbye.

"Easy, guys. I can handle this," Milo says to the two men in the front seat.

I don't let my eyes dart around to see the men behind me, their guns trained on me I'm sure. I keep my focus on slicing the knife into Milo's neck. I should have already done it, instead of waiting to persuade Milo to set me free.

"You are a spirited one. I'm going to have so much fun breaking you."

"You won't touch me."

He tilts his head, allowing me better access to his neck, and I press harder—until one droplet of blood coats the knife.

So close. Just a little harder and blood will be spurting.

Milo chuckles. "You should have slit my throat by now."

I press harder, watching more blood. "And if I slit your throat, your men will kill me a second later."

"Ah, that's your concern." He looks up to his men. "If she slits my throat, you are to do nothing to her. You don't touch her. Understand?"

"Yes, sir," both men say.

I freeze. *What the hell?*

"There, now you are free to slit my throat without any repercussion from my men."

Do it.

"But, you better make sure you kill me when you slice my throat. Because I will make you pay ten times over for any damage you do to me."

His hand comes to my wrist gripping the knife, and he presses it harder to his neck as more blood spills. He doesn't show the slightest sign of agony at the blade's touch. This man understands pain. And this isn't pain to him—I understand the feeling.

"I want you to slice my neck. It will make it so much more fun when I slice your neck right back."

Shit.

What am I doing? I will never get out of here alive. *I don't have to. I just can't get on that yacht.*

He releases his grip on my wrist. "What's it going to be, whore? Slice my neck and see what happens. Because as much as you think you will be able to kill me, you have to slice a lot deeper for me to bleed out before my team of men jumps in to save me."

My eyes cut to the two men driving and the dozens of cars around us. No doubt one of them is a doctor, and no doubt he is carrying a pint of his blood. I've seen what money can do to motivate a doctor to save a dying man's life. Zeke shouldn't be alive except for having the highest paid doctor with the best training to do whatever it takes to save him.

Milo will be no different. One slice won't be enough to kill him. I would need a dozen or more stabs. And Milo will only let me get one before he fights back.

His eyes threaten me, as if they already know my thoughts, and he's a dozen steps ahead of me.

I need to do something he isn't expecting. It's my only chance.

I could stab myself—put an end to this.

I won't.

I want to live.

For no other reason than to kick Enzo's ass for selling me.

There are six additional cars. More than a dozen men ride in the fancy, most likely bulletproof, vehicles all around us. I'm outnumbered by a ridiculous amount.

Milo's phone rings again, but he ignores it—too infatu-ated by what I'm going to do.

I'm going to crash this motherfucking car.

I pull the knife back and slice across Milo's cheek, needing to cause him some pain for thinking he could buy me like prop-erty. And then I fling the knife with everything I can toward the driver. Hoping to God it hits him hard enough for him to lose control of the vehicle. And then I launch myself at him.

The car lurches as I hoped. The knife lands in his shoul-der, and he gasps as my body flings over to him. I grab for the wheel, pulling hard to the right as the car starts spinning.

Yes! This could work!

And then I feel the hands. One pair grabs one arm while another pair grabs the other, pulling me off the man and shoving me into the back seat.

The driver regains control, as the man in the passenger seat pulls the knife out of his back.

The driver curses as the knife is jerked free. Obviously, he isn't as used to dealing with pain as Milo or me.

Milo shoves me down onto the seat, forcing my arms over my head, as his body crushes me down into the black leather.

He's sweating, and a thin line of blood scars his cheek. It may not have caused much damage, but the scar will remain for the rest of his life. A constant reminder on his face of me, at least until I find a way to kill him.

"You okay, Vito?" Milo asks, not taking his heated eyes off of me to check on his driver.

"Yes, it just hurts like a motherfucker," Vito answers.

I don't look away from Milo, but I'm sure Vito is giving me an evil glare.

"Don't worry, Vito; I'll make sure she pays for her crimes."

Milo pulls another knife from his pocket and pushes it against my neck in the same way I did to him earlier.

I hold my breath, trying to remain as still as possible, but I don't let the fear in. I won't. He doesn't deserve my fear.

"How far are we from the yacht?" Milo asks his driver.

"Five minutes."

Five minutes, that's nothing. Once I'm on that yacht, I'll have no hope of getting off. And have no hope of hiding my fear.

"Do it. Slice my pretty neck. I deserve it," I taunt him.

He grins, pushing his weight further into my chest until I can barely breathe. His cock sinks between my legs, and it takes everything inside me not to try and pull away in disgust.

"Do it," I say again. My eyes glaze with a fire to have control over this man. Even if it's just to get him to hurt me, he'll hurt me because of what I did, and what I said. If it weren't for me, he'd still be yelling into his phone. I have control.

"With pleasure," Milo says.

The knife presses hard against my throat, and I feel the warmth of my blood trickling down my cool neck.

He won't kill me. I know that much. He needs me alive to torture me later. Even though a part of me wishes he would kill me and put an end to this.

Everything starts to move in slow motion.

The knife slices deeper, until I can't contain the pain. I grit my teeth to try to keep it in, but the pain is unexpected. *Maybe he is trying to kill me?*

The car is spinning the next second. Milo flies from my body, slamming into the back of the driver's seat.

Vito grips the wheel hard, trying to regain control, but we keep whirling.

I grab my neck and feel the blood soaking my hand as my body grows colder.

Glass shatters.

And then everything stops.

The car.

The screams.

The guns.

I'm cold—so fucking cold. It's been a long time since I felt this level of ice hardening my veins.

I don't move. I let the ice consume me, freezing me in place. Soon I'll be a statue again. I'm sinking back into my shell, and I welcome it if it keeps me alive.

My eyes start fluttering closed, until I see men with guns standing over me. Men I don't recognize. Men with evil and wickedness in their eyes.

Fuck, it's just my luck. To get stolen from Milo only to deal with worse men. And Enzo won't have a fucking clue he has to steal me from this new enemy, that I'm no longer with Milo. I've been taken by new men.

I let my eyes drift closed, and hope I'll never open them again. Death has to be better than this.

4

ENZO

Kai's alive.

And Rowan Evan's men now have her, just as planned. *Thank fuck.*

"They have her," I say, ending the call as I look at Langston and Zeke.

Westcott enters my office a second later. "Is she?"

Even Westcott is worried about Kai.

"She's safe."

Westcott nods. "Do you need anything, sir?"

Langston glares at me, ensuring that I do what I must instead of what I want to do.

"Yes, have my car brought around."

Westcott nods and then leaves. The plan is for me to be seen at Surrender—as publicly as possible for the next hour or so. So that when Milo tries to figure out where Kai is, he won't suspect I took her. He will put all of the blame on Rowan. It's going to kill me and be absolute torture to not be here when Kai returns, but it will be safer for her if Milo doesn't know who has her.

Rowan was more than happy to help us out as soon as I

asked for his help. I claimed I too was an enemy of Milo, which is now true. And I wanted to punish him for crossing me. That the woman he harbored was important to him, so I wanted to steal her back.

I offered Rowan the ten million Milo gave to me for his services. In exchange, he gives me Kai unharmed.

My phone buzzes again. It's Rowan. I still. *Why would he call me back?* Langston and Zeke are supposed to meet his men in half an hour to make the trade.

"Hello," I answer the phone cautiously.

"We don't want to alarm you, but the girl has been hurt."

"What? I told you she wasn't supposed to get hurt. That was the deal."

"It happened before we arrived. The bastard had a knife to her throat."

"Is she?" I can't bring myself to ask if she's alive. If she's dying right now in the back of one of their cars.

"She's alive. She'll survive. Your girl is a fighter. She went into some type of shock, her body shut down, and it seemed to minimize the bleeding. We already have her stitched up. She should have lost a lot more blood than she did. If her body hadn't taken over, that bastard would have killed her."

"Fuck," I breathe.

How could I have been so stupid?

How could I have thought she would be safe for even a second with that monster?

How could I have ever thought it was okay to punish her by selling her? Even if I thought somewhere deep down she wanted him?

How could I?

"We just wanted to let you know so you could have a doctor ready to look her over. Her blood pressure is low, her pulse and breathing are weak, but she's alive. She hasn't woken up yet."

"I'll have a doctor with me to retrieve her."

"Good. Also wanted to let you know we don't want your money."

"Why not?"

"We do some shitty, evil things to make money, same as you. But we don't hurt women; we don't hurt the innocent. It's one rule we never break and never tolerate. It's why we hate Milo so much. He has no respect for women. This I will do for free."

"Thank you. If you need any help putting Milo in his place let me know, I'd be more than happy to help," I say, squeezing the phone hard, knowing how badly I want to hurt Milo myself.

"Of course."

We hang up.

"Change of plan. I'm not going to Surrender. I'm going with you to pick up Kai."

"But—"

"I don't care if Milo finds out I stole her back. He fucking hurt her."

Langston and Zeke's eyes grow big with pain.

"No one touches what's mine. This is my fuck up. And I'm going to fucking fix it."

———

WE MEET Rowan and his men in a back alley. It's still daylight, but I doubt anyone will give us much attention.

I step out of the car and race over to the open door of the Escalade.

Kai.

"She's alive," Rowan says. I'm surprised he helped deliver her himself. This thing between him and Milo is personal.

"Thank you," I say, holding back tears and anger.

I lift her limp body out of the car, and then run back to mine. I brought Dr. Patten with us to help take care of her on the way back. Langston and Zeke are driving in the front.

As soon as we are in the car, Langston takes off like we are an ambulance racing to the hospital.

I see the large cut on her neck, now tied together with stitches as I lay her head in my lap.

Dr. Patten starts checking her vitals, takes her blood pressure, and examines the wound.

"Should I head toward a hospital or home?" Langston asks as he drives.

I look to the doctor to determine Kai's condition.

"The cut looks worse than it is. It's stitched up nicely. Her vitals are slower than normal, but I think it's just because her body went into a survival state. Not because she's at risk of dying. The only thing they could do is give her blood, but I don't think she lost much. There isn't much on her clothing or hair. And her cheeks are still pink."

"Rowan said she didn't lose much blood from what he could tell."

"Good, I think all she needs is rest and time."

"Home, Langston."

I stroke her hair. "I'm so sorry. I'm so fucking sorry. Never again. Never."

I repeat over and over as Langston drives us home. And I don't care who hears or knows what I'm thinking. Kai is too important to risk ever again.

She will never forgive me for this.

I will never forgive myself for this.

But I can ensure it will never happen again. I will do everything I can to protect her. Even if it kills me.

———

As we pull up to the house, Kai opens her eyes. As if she was waiting to feel truly safe before she came back to the world.

She blinks rapidly as she looks at me.

"Enzo?" She croaks. Her voice sounds scratchy, and she winces at the pain.

"Shh, don't talk. You're safe."

Her eyes are immense as she looks at me like she can't believe I'm really here.

The doctor smiles. "I'm glad you are awake Miss Miller. Would you like some pain medication for that neck?" He reaches down to produce a couple of pain pills and a water bottle from his bag.

I take the pills and hold them up to her lips. She takes them, and then I carefully pour water through her parted lips.

"You'll make a full recovery soon. You just need to rest. By tomorrow you should feel a lot better."

"What—" she starts.

I press a finger to her lips.

"Don't use your voice to ask me questions."

I can read her eyes and body well enough to know what she's going to ask anyway.

"We found Milo's closest enemy and hired them to get you out before you got to the yacht. We didn't want Milo knowing we were the ones to get you because we were afraid Milo would attack us and try to get you back. I vowed to protect you, and so I will. Even if I failed you now."

Her pupils dilate before turning small.

"Yes, I had every man I know with a connection to Milo call his phone with various questions—problems with the yacht, questions about partnerships, money transfers, weapons that were supposed to be delivered to him, anything I could to keep him occupied and you safe."

She nods a thanks.

"Don't you dare thank me. Don't thank any of my men or Rowan's men. We should be protecting people that deserve it. And you, beautiful, deserve every inch of our protection. You deserve so much more than I can give you."

"I'm so sorry he hurt you," I stroke her neck where a permanent scar will serve as another reminder of the pain, just like all the other marks on her body.

Her eyes shine, and I realize what she's trying to say. She's not sad about the scar. It's a good reminder. A reminder of something she did to Milo.

I smile. "You hurt him first?"

She nods.

"Good girl. Where?"

She points to her cheek and makes a long line. She's vicious when she needs to be.

I hate that her fighting back almost cost her her life. But I know she's truly healed if she was able to fight instead of locking herself inside.

"You are so incredible." I stroke her forehead and hair. Even though we are stopped outside the house, none of us are in any hurry to go inside. All eyes in the car are on Kai, soaking up everything she tells us with her body.

She looks to Langston in the driver seat and points to his shoulder.

He smiles at her. "You got the driver in the shoulder?"

She nods.

"That's my girl," Langston says.

I shoot him a look when Langston says *my girl*. But he simply raises his eyebrows as if to say Kai's as much his as she is mine. She may be calm and understanding right now, but the second she gets her strength back, she will be fucking ready to kill me for getting her into this mess in the first place. Even though I ensured her safe return, it doesn't matter. I fucked up in the worst possible way.

The absolute worst way. And I deserve every bit of her revenge coming my way later.

She looks around the car smiling at each of us, showing her thanks and gratitude for getting back. When her eyes arrive back on mine, she smiles for a split second before letting it drop. And I know that's the last smile I will be getting.

"I promise you—never again. I will die before I let another man hurt you. I will die before I let another man take you. I will give up everything to you if that will save you. I don't care how you hurt or betray me in the future. You have my allegiance. If you win the empire, I will spend my life serving you and protecting you. I'll even give up the empire to you now, if that's what you want. I'll lose every round until you are Black. And I will spend the rest of my life keeping you safe."

She bites her lip as she studies my distraught face, and I know what she's asking me. She doesn't want to be Black. She wants what she's always wanted. The one thing I'm desperate to give her and not sure I can. She wants her freedom.

"What?" Zeke asks, looking from her to me, not understanding.

"Kai wants me to set her free."

Zeke's face falls heavy. "You can't. It's not safe. Definitely not now that Milo will be doing everything possible, including burning this city down, to get Kai back."

My eyes cut to Zeke, silencing him and the rest of the car. Because his words aren't helpful even though they are the truth.

"You will be free as soon as it's safe. I will take you wherever you want to go. I will give you the ten million Milo paid me in the sale. I will give you everything you want. I just can't let you go yet. I'm sorry. I won't let you get hurt again. But I'll give you as much freedom as I can while you're here. I hope it's enough."

She sucks in a breath and looks around at all of the eyes on her, and I know it will never be enough.

"So I'm trapped here until you can determine it's safe for me?" she asks, her voice weak.

"Yes," I say, my heart breaking.

"Then I'll be trapped here forever because I'll never be safe."

5

KAI

IT HURTS TO THINK. The muscles twinge every time I make my neck move, but hopefully, the pain medications will kick in soon, because I have a lot to say to Enzo, and it can't wait.

I'm trapped here. That much I know. Enzo will never let me go until he can ensure my protection, something he will never be able to do. Milo will start hunting me as soon as he tends to his wounds. All of Enzo's enemies have now become mine. Whether the news of our fake marriage spread, or realizing I'm the daughter of a Miller and I have as much right to the empire as Enzo does. The world knows of my existence and will be coming for me.

Enzo continues to stroke my hair, looking down at me like he's terrified of living if I were to die. I've seen something close to this on his face before, but never *this*.

Something changed when Milo took me. Enzo felt pain when I was taken. *Maybe Enzo does have a heart?*

How can I be happy and pissed at someone at the same time? I feel both emotions in equal measures. I'm livid Enzo sold me and got me into this situation in the first place. And

I'm elated he saved me. I'm happy he's scared to lose me. I'm thrilled he offered to give everything to me in payment.

He offered everything but my freedom.

Enzo nods and all the men file out of the car.

Langston opens Enzo's door. Slowly Enzo eases out from underneath me, stands, and then his arms are under me scooping me out.

I can walk, I say with my eyes because it's not important enough to speak with my voice and cause myself pain.

"I know you can, brave girl. But you shouldn't have to. I'll be your legs forever if you let me. I'll be your armor. Your fighter. Your protector. Watching you walk out the door took something from me. I don't understand why seeing you go hurt so badly, but it did. Worse than being shot. I won't let it happen again."

I soak in his words. *Truth.* His words are the truth.

He smiles, continuing to read my mind.

I don't ever have to worry about Enzo hurting me again. He won't, even in the game. I'm safe from his wrath.

Enzo carries me up to the bedroom where all the men have gathered. All of their concern is still etched on their faces.

I shake my head with a bashful grin as Enzo lays me down on the bed.

He sighs. "They just need to make sure you are okay. If you weren't, you can count on the fact Langston and Zeke would kill me themselves."

"You okay, stingray?" Zeke asks.

Stingray? I raise an eyebrow.

"Yea, it's your nickname now. We needed a code name for you during the mission. That's what I came up with. Because you pack a punch like stingrays, and you come from the sea."

I reach out, needing to squeeze Zeke's hand. He looks at it in fear.

"It's okay," I whisper. We both need the touch. He finally walks to the bed and takes it, and then I pull him to me so he can hug me. The familiar jolt of energy shoots through me at the touch, but I don't focus on it. I focus on this man who cares about me. Something I don't think I've ever experienced. My own father didn't even care about me.

When Zeke releases me, I look to Langston. I tell him to come here with my eyes. He does and hugs me the same way Zeke did. Two men that care about me. *How did I get so lucky?*

And then I see Enzo. His look is both similar and different from Langston and Zeke's. He cares, but there is something else there I can't place.

Zeke and Langston leave, as Dr. Patten starts examining my wound one more time. He puts a dressing over it and gives me a bottle of painkillers to take. He reminds me to take it easy for a day or two, but I should heal easily. The stitches can come out in two weeks.

And then it's Enzo and me alone in the bedroom we share. And as much as I'm trapped, I don't feel that way— I'm home.

Fuck, it's messed up that the only place I've ever considered home is this house.

Enzo sits on the edge of the bed while I study him. He's lost in thought. His brow has deepened, and the lines near his eyes have creased. I'm sure he's thinking about how to keep me safe from Milo.

Milo will be coming. But it will take some time for him to realize Enzo has me, and not his other enemies. We are safe enough for now.

Right now, I need something different. I know the

doctor ordered rest, but I won't be able to rest until I get what I need.

I need to solidify Enzo's promise. I need to heal. And I need to know I will never be hurt by this man again.

Enzo reads my thoughts. He knows what I need. But I think he's going to fight me on it. I think he's going to say I need rest first. I need to sleep.

However, Enzo surprises me as usual.

"Punish me. It will make you feel better. And when it's done, I will spend the rest of my life earning every bit of your trust."

6

ENZO

Kai needs rest. She needs to heal. She's been through hell today. She's barely recovered from her first encounter with Milo. He only cut her neck this time, but it's enough. Enough to bring back all the painful memories she experienced for years.

And it's all my fault.

I may have thought I was setting her free by selling her to Milo, but it was selfish. I knew even if she wanted to be with Milo that it would hurt her to be sold to another man. I knew by giving her to him, I would win Black. Milo would never let her leave his side long enough to come back and compete for this empire.

I thought it was the best solution. Instead of the nightmare it has become.

Kai needs to rest, but she needs revenge more. She needs to make me pay for the pain I've caused her.

I don't blame her. I know how it feels to feel helpless to the pain—to the anger. She needs me to suffer as she's suffering. When Zeke was hurt because of Kai, all I could do was get his revenge. I couldn't think—the pain clouded my head so deeply. And when I thought Kai had betrayed me by wanting Milo instead of me, all I saw was red.

Kai needs to punish me. She needs to let go of her anger. It's the only way we will ever have a shot at moving past this.

I stand up and meet Kai's gaze. Knowing in my heart we both need this more than we need air right now.

"What do you need?"

Her face scrunches in confusion. "What do you mean?"

"A whip? A knife? Chains? A gun? What?"

Please, anything but a gun. I vowed I would never let anyone shoot me again without fighting back. And I would have to break that promise to myself.

Kai studies me for a moment, as if trying to determine which method of torture she should use.

She shakes her head and pats the empty space on the bed beside her.

"You sure?" I ask.

She nods.

Fuck.

Somehow not using any weapons seems scarier than using one. I think back to the last time she hurt me with her body—forcing me to take something from her so savagely. I won't let that happen again.

I slowly walk around the side of the bed and lie down next to her, my hands folded over my chest, staring up at the ceiling.

I'm not used to following orders. But today, I will do anything she asks, including slitting my own throat if that's what she needs.

I wait.

But she doesn't speak. She doesn't move.

The waiting stretches, driving me mad with what she

could be thinking. But I don't dare open my mouth. I don't ask her to move things along faster. This is about her.

Healing her.

Letting go of her pain.

And living through the anger.

I want to close my eyes to shut out the silence, but I don't even allow myself to do that.

I wait.

I suffer.

And then I wait some more.

Finally, I feel her cold fingers brush against mine.

I turn my head to face her. But I don't see the look of wrath I was expecting.

I see fear.

"Kai? Did something happen? Are you okay?" I ask, suddenly worried. I try to roll to her, to understand what's happening.

She puts a hand up, pressing against my chest, stopping me from touching her.

The cold chill shoots through me. I shudder at how cold I feel. Usually, the cold settles my heat, calming me and making me feel whole. But this time, it empties me.

Kai looks at me unblinking. And that's when I realize what's happening. She won't punish me with whips or beatings. She will punish me by showing me everything she's feeling and everything she's ever felt.

I will feel all of her pain. It will be impossible for me not to. The connection we share is too deep not to. I won't be able to shut it out like she does. And I'll never forget the pain.

The torment she has gone through.

Kai releases my hand and then moves her fingers to her neck where the doctor put the dressing. She removes the dressing. And I truly stare at the fresh wound for the first time. I could hardly look at it in the car except to ensure she was still alive.

She takes my hand again and moves it toward her neck.

"No," I say, not wanting to hurt her or disturb the stitches. Like my touch might infect the wound in some way.

She holds my gaze, and her lips tighten. I know she won't let me get away with not doing this. She carefully places my hand over the wound.

It's hot as fire. The only part of her body that isn't cold. And I can't imagine what that feels like to her. Not only does her neck hurt, but it feels like she was branded with sizzling flames.

I close my eyes, and I can feel the sharp blade pressing against her skin. I feel the searing blood warming her much cooler skin. I feel the terror pulsing through her veins as blood spills and knowing the only way to stop it was to shut herself down. Knowing every time she shuts down, it takes a mountain of pain to reenter the world again.

She holds in her tears, but I can't mine. I let a tear fall.

She growls at the sight of my weakness. And I suck the rest in. I pull my hand back, needing relief from the pain and loneliness.

No, she mouths—her face stern.

She grabs my hand again and traces the bruises on her face with my fingertips. The thin lines on her face that will continue to soften with time, but never disappear completely. Most of the scars aren't my fault. They are her father's for selling her the first time. But this is what would have happened again to her if I didn't stop Milo from taking her.

She lets go of my hand for a second and then removes her shirt, lifting it up over her head.

I wince at the discoloration of her skin. Purples, blues, and yellows cover her body, in much the same way her skin was when she first arrived.

I should kill Milo for what he did to her—I will kill him.

She takes my hand and moves my fingers over her broken and beaten skin. And with each touch, it's like a knife is being shoved into my own flesh. I can't imagine the amount of suffering she endured. I've lived with her for months now. But this, knowing I almost sent her to endure this again, it's too much.

Tears fall as I feel everything and realize how much it would break me to see her suffer for even a second.

I feel the cold.

I feel the pain.

I feel the loneliness.

"Here," she moves my hand over her shoulder to a mark I know. A similar mark to several I wear at the hands of my father.

"Here I was shot because I wouldn't willingly suck Jarod's cock. I bled for days. The wound became infected. I became delirious, sick with fever."

I relive my own bullet wound. I know the pain. I remember the blood that never seemed to stop pouring out of me until I was too weak to stand. And she's suffered worse.

"Here." She moves my hand to her ribcage. "Milo beat me until it burned to breathe. He broke ribs that have been broken numerous times before."

Jesus.

She sucks in a breath, and I can see the pain. Not from the wound on her neck. But I see how her lungs move

45

cautiously, never pulling in a full breath of oxygen to avoid expanding her lungs as little as possible.

"The worst was here." She forces my hand down to her lower abdomen. "I was stabbed here so many times. The pain always made me wretch. But worst of all, I faced the fact that I couldn't help but thinking each stab was going into my ovaries, my uterus. I might not be able to ever have kids because of these stabs." A tiny sob escapes. "But at the same time, I begged for them to keep stabbing, because I never wanted the ability to have kids and bring a child into such a cruel world."

She rips my hand from her body.

"You may have fixed your error, but it doesn't mean I can ever forget what happened."

She shoves me back against the bed, and then her body is straddling mine. She's reaching back, and I know instinctively what she is reaching for.

She doesn't need it. I will say and do whatever she wants, but she needs to feel the power of holding the sharp metal in her hand.

Kai grabs the knife from my ankle and then presses it hard against my neck.

Adrenaline drills through my body in spades. Not because I truly fear for my life, I know Kai won't kill me even if I deserve it, but my body reactions to the threat all the same. I grip the sheets to force myself from retaliating. It takes all of my restraint to keep myself planted on the bed instead of disarming her.

Her eyes engulf me, and a sly smile curls on her lips.

"Why?" she asks.

"You already know why," I breathe, careful not to move my throat much to prevent the knife from dragging deeper into my neck.

"I know why, but do you? You say you sold me because I betrayed you, but that's not the truth. Tell me the truth."

"It is the truth."

"No, I don't owe you my loyalty. We are enemies. We are playing a game that generations of our families have played before. You own me. It shouldn't have mattered to you that I slept with another man to win the game. It wouldn't have been a betrayal."

My nostrils flare, and I see red as I think about her with another man.

"You're mine," I curse, rolling us over so I'm on top. The knife is still pressed to my neck, but it doesn't matter. It doesn't matter who is in control anymore. It matters she realizes that even though we are enemies, she is still fucking mine.

She glares like a dragon breathing fire at me. "I'm not yours, not in the way you want."

I lower my mouth, hovering over her tender pink lips. She keeps the knife pressing against my carotid artery, like that is going to keep me from claiming her.

"Admit it," she raises her eyebrows, her confidence never as great as it is in this moment.

"No."

I feel the warm blood draining from my neck, but I know it's nothing more than a nick. She doesn't want me to bleed, at least not from my neck. She wants me to bleed from my heart. But she forgets I don't have a heart. I'm incapable of feeling anything.

Yes, I want to protect her, but in the same way I want to protect my favorite car from getting stolen. She belongs to me, not anyone else. That's all this is.

"You have a heart." Kai trails the blade down my neck, over my shirt, to my chest. She stops it over my heart.

"My heart hardened, years ago. You learned to shut down to survive; I learned to shut off my feelings."

"And you brought me back from my darkest cavern. I was trapped inside the darkness, and you showed me how to live in the light. You may have shut off your heart to protect it, but it's starting to thaw."

"You can't thaw it. You're made of ice."

"And you're fire, but it's going to take more than fire to free your heart."

"I don't want it freed."

She grits her teeth as she pushes the knife harder against my chest until I can feel the metal against my skin. Until I feel the pierce of the blade over my heart. All I have to do to get the pain to stop is lean back, but it would mean removing myself from Kai. I need to feel every inch of her. I want more, not less. I want to shove my tongue so deep into her throat that I taste all of her. I want to nibble and attack her precious neck so the long cut on her neck is nothing in comparison to the marks I leave. I want to spread her legs, throwing them over my head until her thighs are trying to suffocate me as I lick her into oblivion.

"Admit it, you care about me."

"Only as a man cares about his car."

"I'm not an object."

"No, you are the bane of my existence."

"Admit it, Black," Kai says. She never calls me Black. It would be admitting defeat. That I'm the true ruler.

"Not until you admit you like being trapped here. You like my protection."

She pants against my lips. If she wants me to admit I want her, then she has to admit she wants me. That she doesn't feel like a prisoner. That she wants to be here.

We both lock in our determination to not admit defeat.

Because that is what it would feel like: *defeat*. We are both too strong to ever develop any sort of feelings toward each other.

"I've already thawed as much of your heart as I'm going to without your help. It's your move Black," Kai says.

I lean down and finally taste the lips of the woman I've claimed, stolen, sold, broke, healed, and cried over. Somehow the tears I shed before is what breaks through all the rest for me. I don't cry. *Ever.* Not since I was a boy. And then when I'm around Kai, I cry all the time for her. It's just because her life is so tragic.

"You care about me. Truth or lie?" Kai says.

"Truth," I breathe, as I brush our lips together again, my salty fire mixing with her sweet cold.

"You like me. Truth or lie?"

"Truth."

I dip my tongue between her parted lips and both our bodies ease. Her muscles melt against the kiss.

"You like being mine. Truth or lie?" I say.

"Truth," she whispers, pulling my bottom lip into her mouth.

She drops the knife, and I push it off the bed, as I tangle my body with hers. I taste her deeply, our teeth clash, and our temperatures slam together, as we stop fighting with our words and instead fight with our tongues.

Kai grips my shirt, thrusting it up my body over my six pack and then jerks it forcefully from my body. I lay my body on top of her, melting her exterior. But I want more than just the surface. I want all of her. Kai's right, I want as deep as it gets when it comes to her. I just don't think I can give anything in return. But I want her to depend on me, beg for me, live for me.

We shouldn't be making out right now. We are both too

angry. In too much pain for this to be the logical next step. Kai should be healing, and I should be finding a way to keep Milo from figuring out I have Kai.

Instead, we devour each other. I'm not careful with her like I should be. She's bruised and physically broken, but fierceness inside her has only grown stronger. It's the main reason why I like her as Kai says I do.

And the way she's biting as much as she's kissing me, I know she doesn't want this easy and gentle. She wants me to push her, show her how desperate I am for her. That was her plan all along, and I fell for it. She may think she tricked me as she did before, but it's not tricking if I'm doing it willingly.

"Does it hurt?" she asks as she kisses my neck where she spilled some of my blood.

"No."

She shakes her head as she bites over my chest and to my heart.

"That's not what I mean."

I cock my head, but I don't want to know what she means. She's dangerous right now.

I grab her neck; she winces as I brush my hand over her wound. I push my hand back, fisting her hair as I claim her mouth. As long as I'm kissing her, she can't speak. She can't do any more damage. And neither can I because when we are together like this—our bodies mixing in a hurricane of temperatures and moans is when we are most right. It's where we are most meant to be.

I like Kai Miller.

I like the fucking.

I like how she makes me fight for her.

I like how nothing is easy, and yet everything is easy at the same time.

I like how it feels to have her in my arms. Her body temperature may be cooler than mine, but it doesn't feel that way to me. It feels like a breath of air when I touch her, grounding me, while also giving me wings to fly.

I hook my thumbs into her pants and pull them down. And then I drop my head between her legs. Her body instantly arches as I find her clit with my tongue. I growl, the vibration in my throat sending shockwaves through her body.

"Jesus, Black."

I tighten my grip on her clit with my teeth, applying just enough pressure to drive her mad. Good thing she doesn't still have the knife, or she'd use it to threaten me to stop teasing her.

"Yes," she moans.

God, I love her voice.

I flick my tongue over and over. I feel her hands grab my hair, but she doesn't get to touch. I grab her wrists and force them apart, glued to the bed.

All I want is for her to feel my tongue on her most sensitive of areas. For her to remember I'm the only man who has touched her here. The only man who gets to hear her cries as she comes.

"Wait...I want your cock," she pulls her hands, trying to loosen them from my grip.

I drive my tongue into her cunt, pulling her juices out and lapping over her clit.

"And you shall have it, but first. *This*. I want to feel your first explosion rattle the entire room."

Kai pants at my words, as if my words are causing the orgasm instead of my tongue. Faster I pull her under my spell. Taunting her, teasing her, until I finally give her the pressure she needs, and she finally gives me what I want—

my name in as much of a prayer as a curse falling from her beautiful lips.

"Enzo!"

Her body shakes viciously, her thighs clench as I pull an orgasm from her body. But that was just to prepare her for round two. I might not deserve to sink my cock inside her, but it's not about deserving. It's about need. And we both need it more than we need blood to keep pumping in our veins.

I pull the condom from my pocket and barely get my pants down and the condom on before I explode like a teenage boy.

I grab her and roll her on top, so I don't completely crush her underneath me, and she continues to have some control.

She straddles me with flushed cheeks, and heavy eyes. She claws at my chest as I pull her down on top of my sheathed cock.

Each time we fuck I still can't believe how tight she is. But there is no pain on her face. I slide in easily from her slickness.

She rides me hard, and I'm sure the good doctor would yell at us both for this, but it's worth it. I'd gladly give her all my blood to keep her alive after this and die a happy man.

I thrust into her as she grinds on top of me, her clit angling toward my hard stomach.

I roll my head back for a second before reminding myself to focus on the beautiful woman humping me. Because someday, she won't be mine anymore.

Kai puts her hand over my heart as we pump harder.

"Here, it hurts here," she says.

My eyes are defiant, but there is no use in hiding it. "Just fuck me, beautiful."

She leans down, still riding me but at a slower pace as our foreheads touch.

"You love me. Truth or lies?" this sentence comes out as question more than any of her previous ones. This one she doesn't know the answer to before she asks it. She knows I care about her. I even like her. But love, that's on a whole different level.

"I love it when you scream my name when you come," I wink at her. Thrusting again to try to get us off this topic. But she's determined. She wants a real answer.

"That's not what I mean. Do you love me? Do you have a heart? Are you capable of loving?" she presses against my heart with her palm.

"Do you love me?" I ask.

"Can a slave ever love her master?" she says back.

"Can a predator ever love his prey?" I snap back.

Her face grows determined. She wants me to admit weakness. Admit I love her when she could never love me in return.

"I'm not capable of love, Kai. We are fucking, nothing more. I care about you sure. I want to protect you and keep you alive because I want to protect the broken. But when this is over, when one of us is declared Black, this is over. You want to be free; I'll find a way to make it happen the second this twisted game is through."

"You're too evil for love, and I'm too broken." She smiles sadly. "Just making sure before you start proposing to me for real."

I chuckle and kiss her lips. "You don't have to worry about that. This is the best we will ever have, with anyone. Neither of us can love. Neither wants to get married. Neither wants to start a family. But this connection we have. It's special. And it's real. And it can be the best damn thing we have. Because not being capable of falling in love is the best damn gift either of us has ever received."

She nods. "Fuck me and remind me what I have instead of what I'm giving up."

So I do. I fuck her hard, quickly moving back into our rhythm together. Our blood pumps, and it might as well be flowing through me to her as in sync we both are together.

I drive in harder.

"You like that, baby?"

"Fuck, yes."

"You have nothing to fear. You're safe—always."

I fuck her harder. Deeper. Longer. Until I know we are both going to spend the next few hours passed out in the bed from a sex coma instead of what I need to be doing—finding a way to protect her.

She screams and pants her orgasm out until her screams turn into silent pleas. A single tear rolls down her cheek.

I kiss it away, hoping with its removal so too am I removing her pain and her anger. I know we aren't capable of forgiveness any more than we are capable of love. But we are capable of moving forward no matter what. We are survivors.

We collapse on the bed next to each other. We both pant hard, and I'm too tired to get up to even remove the condom.

We both close our eyes as sleep begins to come for us. But not before I realize what I have to do to keep her safe. And she isn't going to like it.

7

KAI

I love Enzo Black.

I love him.

I shouldn't. It should be the last feeling I ever feel. But I do. I love him. I thought I was too broken for love. I thought I was undeserving. But nobody told my heart any of those things.

Enzo is cruel. He's dangerous. He's evil.

He sold me, but not out of malice, but because he loves me too, and it hurt him too much to imagine me with another man. It hurt so fucking much he had to get rid of me. He needed me gone in order to survive.

But he's so broken he will never admit he's capable of love.

Love is weak.

Love is fear.

Love is dangerous.

I understand, it's how I feel. I've never felt so vulnerable as I do now—loving him.

I didn't want to admit it to myself. He's evil incarnate.

But it doesn't matter. Because he's my evil, and I'm his broken.

And I'm completely fucked. Because as much as I love Enzo, he will never admit his love back. He will never show his love beyond protecting me, beyond claiming me as his.

I thought that could be enough, being his. But my heart is already pierced by his confession. He doesn't love me. He's willing to give me up when this is over.

Enzo deserves to be Black. I already think of him as Black. But I will fight every day to prolong the game as long as possible. Because the longer the game lasts, the longer I get Enzo. And I need him, forever.

I need him to love me like I love him.

I'm only just learning what love means. It's the first time, I've admitted it to myself. I thought I wasn't capable of love. But maybe because I'm not capable of loving someone who isn't broken. And Enzo is as broken as it comes. His life has been just as tortuous as mine.

I should end it. Give him peace. Let him win what he deserves. I spent six years being tortured. He's spent his entire life. But I'm selfish. I want him. I love him. And if I only get a few more months to love him, then so be it. I'll take it. I just won't ever admit it. Because admitting my feelings out loud would hurt worse than keeping them inside.

I've forgiven him for hurting me, which only verifies my feelings for him. Only my love for him could allow me to forgive him for the sins he's committed against me. And these feelings are going to screw me over more than anything else.

I've been tortured, abused, shot, but I've never had a broken heart. Never had love ripped from me. And I know that's where our journey ends. With my heart bleeding for him.

Enzo stirs. His body is draped over me, warming me more than any blanket or heater ever could. I never liked fire, never liked being hot living in the Miami sun, but with Enzo I welcome it.

He smiles at me.

"You're sticky," I say with a smile. The condom fell off sometime while we were sleeping and his cum now sticks to my thigh.

"You complaining?"

I stretch. "I guess not." I smile wider. I'll never complain as long as I keep getting sex like that. It wasn't my intention when we started. I just wanted him to under-stand how serious this is to me. This isn't a game. This is my life.

But then I made the mistake of touching him, and that lit a flame neither of us knows how to extinguish.

"Shower with me," he commands instead of asking.

He rolls off me, and the bed dips as he stands up.

I nod and slowly follow. Apparently being in love means I don't mind when he gives me orders. Am I doomed to spend the rest of my time with him meek and weak, merely following orders like a lovesick puppy?

Yes, and I'll be all too happy to do it.

I watch Enzo walk; his tight ass is too hard not to watch as we enter his ginormous bathroom. He starts the shower before tossing the condom in the trash bin.

His eyes are fixed on me, and he stops me to examine my neck wound.

"Does it hurt?" he asks.

I shake my head. Of course it hurts, but it's nothing compared to what I know I will feel when we are over.

He frowns. He knows I'm lying. He drops his hand and disappears into the bedroom, reappearing with two pills and a bottle of water. I take the pills without arguing and then take a sip of water to wash them down.

He nods, satisfied.

And then we step into the shower, neither of us keeping our eyes off each other. We stand close together but don't touch. If he moves, I move, like a dance we orchestrated, instead of a stalemate.

"What are you doing?" I ask, as the water beads down on us.

"Watching you."

I shake my head. "No, you are trying to hide your plan. I think you've kept enough secrets from me. Tell me the plan."

"I don't have a plan."

"Liar."

He sighs. "Can't we just enjoy a shower together?"

"No, because it gives you time to figure out how to hide the truth from me."

He rubs his hands through my hair, washing the long strands, stalling even though it feels nice.

"Enzo..."

"I have a plan, but you are going to hate it."

I suck in a breath, already suspecting what his plan is, but he needs to say it.

"Try me."

"Milo doesn't know I have you, and until I figure out how to deal with him, I think it's best if we keep the fact you are here hidden. I know you won't like that. You are half owner of the Black empire. You have every right to show up at Surrender same as me. But that's why I think it's best that neither of us goes near Surrender for a while. We can run the business from elsewhere. I can show you more of the ropes of how to run things."

"You mean you want to leave on one of the yachts," I say flatly, saying what he's been avoiding this entire time.

"Yes."

8

ENZO

KAI DIDN'T FIGHT me on my plan to board a yacht and sail until Milo is either dead or we have a plan to ensure he will never touch us.

I expected a fight.

I expected a battle.

I expected to have to throw her ass over my shoulder with her kicking and cursing to get her onto a yacht, knowing I can't guarantee when we will touch land again.

I love the sea, so it's no problem to spend years at a time on the ocean. But for Kai, living on the sea is her biggest nightmare.

But she didn't fight me, maybe because she thought it was inevitable. Or maybe because something changed. Being around her feels different. She should be steaming still after what I did. It was unforgivable. I was an idiot. And I know I haven't done enough to make up for it. But she's tolerating me.

More than tolerating me. She beams when I'm around her, and follows my order without argument. I want to ask what's going on, but I don't dare. I need her to do exactly as I say, at least until I get her on that yacht.

I left Kai in the bedroom and sent Westcott to purchase any items she will need and pack up the rest of what she has because I don't know when we will hit land again.

"What's the plan?" Langston asks, his arms crossed as I enter my office. Both him and Zeke continue to scowl at me, and I don't think they will ever stop after what I did to Kai.

"I'll tell you when you wipe that scowl from your face," I answer, as I collapse into my chair behind my desk.

Langston growls. "Not going to happen. Kai is now a member of this family. You decided that the day you brought her here. And yes, she may have fucked up. But you fucked up worse. She's earned my forgiveness; you haven't yet. So I will keep being pissed as long as I want."

I grin at his loyalty to this family. I truly wish Kai was a part of the family as Langston says. It would be nice to have a girl around. She's not though, and can never be. Because as long as I'm Black, she can never join the family, it's too dangerous. And if she were to ever become Black, she would be in constant danger. Not going to happen.

"Glad to know where your loyalties lie, Langston," I say with a huff. I look at Zeke who is crossing his arms smirking down at me. His muscles are twice the size of mine, which should intimidate me—it doesn't. I know behind the muscles is a big softy who cares about me more than he cares about hurting me.

"The plan is we are all getting on the Savage and getting lost in the middle of fucking nowhere, until Rowan takes out Milo or I find a way to kill him myself. In the meantime, we will run the empire and continue the game at sea. I need you both to make the necessary arrangements to get the Savage prepared and ready to go with a full crew in the next hour. Westcott is helping Kai pack. And I need to make a phone call to Liesel."

"Liesel?" Zeke cocks his head. He's always hated her even though he would never say it to my face.

"Yes, Milo knows about Liesel remember? I took her as my date to Milo's party. It isn't safe for Liesel if she stays here. He could kidnap her and interrogate her to get answers about us. She needs to come with us."

Zeke raises an eyebrow. "That woman isn't going to drop her high paying job and come ride around on a yacht all for an unknown amount of time. Not without payment in return."

I know exactly the kind of payment Zeke in insinuating with his comment.

"Liesel isn't like that," I roll my eyes at him. And even if she is, Liesel means too much to me to just leave behind. Even if it will complicate things a bit.

"Whatever you say." Zeke and Langston exchange knowing glances.

"Just get the yacht ready—one hour," I say sternly as both men walk out of my office.

And then I take out my phone and scroll to the number listed as "*My Everything.*"

I really should change that, but she's still my everything. I would never let anyone hurt Liesel. I would fight to the death for her. Kill for her. I have killed for her. Too many times to count.

And she's finally living the life she deserves. She's happy. I don't want to take that away from her. Even if it's to keep her safe. But she doesn't exactly have a choice.

I sigh. I convinced Kai with only a sentence, maybe Liesel will be just as easy.

"Hello, handsome. Didn't get enough at me at the party, huh?" Liesel says seductively into the phone.

I smile. I know she's just teasing. We've dated in the past, but we quickly realized we were better suited as friends than as lovers.

"I need you to do a favor for me," I say, deciding that is the best angle to play with Liesel.

"I already did a favor for you, handsome. I think it's time you do a favor for me. And I know exactly how I want you to repay me. I remember your tongue being especially skilled in the art of licking."

"I have a—" *Wait, was I about to call Kai my girlfriend?* She's anything but. She's my captive for goodness sakes. But it doesn't change how I feel. I don't want to fuck Liesel or any woman other than Kai.

"It's not going to happen, Liesel. You're going to have to figure out a different way for me to repay you, but right now I need to ask another favor."

She practically grins through the phone, but I don't know why. "You like the whore, don't you?"

"She's. Not. A. Whore." If one more person calls Kai a whore, I'm going to turn barbaric. I don't care who it is.

Liesel purrs into the phone. "That's too bad. I would have loved to get into her panties like we used to. Our three-ways were some of my favorite nights with you." She's trying to get me riled up and turned on at the thought of having two women in my bed. Two women that both mean something to me—Liesel and Kai. When Liesel and I were dating, we would try all sorts of crazy things in bed. Three-somes, tying each other up, whips, dildos, every toy imaginable. But I can't imagine needing any of those things with Kai. With Kai, it's different. I don't need all the flashy toys, and I sure as hell am not going to share Kai with Liesel.

I ignore Liesel's last comment.

"I need you to a pack a bag."

"Oh, so this is an overnight booty call."

Ignore her, I tell my temper. I'm trying to save this woman and everyone I care about at the moment, and she is trying to goad me.

"Pack a bag with everything you could possibly need for months. I'll have Langston pick you up within the hour. We are all getting on the Savage, and I don't know when we will make port again."

Silence. For a woman that always has words to say and never shuts up, it's unusual to hear silence.

"Did you hear me, Liesel?"

"Yes," she finally says. "What happened?"

"I don't have time to explain everything, but Milo Wallace happened. I fucked up and betrayed him, and now he will be hunting me and everyone he knows I have a connection with. He'll kill you if he finds you to try and get information on me and to retrieve what he bought from me. So you are going to get your ass on my yacht in the next hour because I don't want to have to worry about your safety. I don't care how many clients are expecting your law skills. You can work from the yacht."

Another pause. *Fucking Liesel, this isn't the time to get silent on me.*

"What did he buy from you?" her voice is soft and quiet as she speaks, and I suspect she already knows the answer.

"Kai, he bought Kai."

More silence, and I know she's judging me. Not for selling Kai to Milo, but for stealing her back. Liesel has always wanted me to be stronger. To stick to my decisions and not look weak. Stealing Kai back, Liesel would see as a weakness.

"Thirty-minutes, Liesel. Langston will be there in thirty minutes." I hang up the phone without waiting for her to confirm she is coming. She will come, if Langston has to drag her ass onto my yacht. I don't care. I'm not leaving her behind for Milo to find.

———

WESTCOTT DRIVES Kai and me to the pier to get on the Savage, my favorite yacht out of the fleet of yachts I own.

I hold Kai's hand the entire time, but I've been on the phone most of the drive dealing with the logistics of getting everyone that matters onto the yacht as quickly as possible, while also ensuring Surrender and the rest of my businesses are running smoothly. But when we pull up in front of the yacht, I drop the call with Langston. He can figure out what needs to be done; Kai is my entire focus.

"Are you okay, baby?"

Kai doesn't react to me calling her baby. It feels natural falling from my lips. As does every other term of endearment I can think of.

Kai's chest rises and falls slowly, as she forces herself to take a deep breath. The sun reflects off her light olive skin and jet black hair. She tucks her long wavy hair behind her ear and shivers in her pale yellow sundress. She needs a jacket, but I'd rather be the one providing her all her warmth.

I scoot closer and put my arms around her shoulders. She leans back into me, accepting my offer to warm up her body.

"You ready for this? If there were any other way, I would do it," I say.

She shakes her head. "No, you wouldn't. There is

another way. We stay and fight instead of running. But it's not about if we should stay and fight or if we should run and hide. You think I need this in order to fully heal. In order to be able to let me go, you need to know that I'm whole. I will never be whole; I can't be. Not anymore. But thank you for trying."

I cup her chin, not accepting she is anything less than whole. Sure, she has more healing she needs to do, but that doesn't change that I think she's pretty amazing as she is.

My lips come down hungrily on hers, determined to wipe away any thoughts that she is less than. I tease her tongue with mine, and suck the oxygen from her lungs, making her feel like enough while also distracting her from what she is going to have to do. Step onto a yacht and not know when it will return to shore—her nightmare.

I want her panties soaked; I want her begging, dying to come before she has to step foot on the yacht. I want her focused on me and my cock—nothing else will be able to distract her.

I hear Westcott step out of the car, giving us at least the illusion of privacy, and then I make my move. I grab her bare thighs, and slide my hand upward, gliding my hand along her shimmering skin.

I move to pull her panties down, when I find none. She's bare.

So. Fucking. Hot.

I want to fuck her right here on the backseat of the Porsche Cayenne. *Thank God, I have great self-control.* Otherwise, I would. And then she'd be spent, but not necessarily distracted.

Focus. You'll have your chance to have her, just wait.

Good thing I believe in delayed gratification.

Kai arches as my fingers dip between her thighs. Her

mouth opens wide in a cry, unable to focus on kissing me when I'm teasing her so tortuously.

"Please, yes," Kai moans.

I kiss her neck, careful not to touch the area that has been recovered with a bandage. And I swear I feel every nerve ending in her body switch on like a light switch. I feel the surge of energy swirling and begging to be set free.

Not yet, my beauty. Not yet.

My hand is soaked with her sweet juices as I taunt her clit with my fingers. I slip one inside to feel just how wet. And I know she is seconds away from squeezing my finger as her orgasm pulses around me. When she is one second away, I stop.

Her head whips to me. "Why did you stop?"

I kiss her plump and swollen lips. "Because I want you thinking about me all damn day. Don't you dare touch yourself. I want to know I can make you come whenever I want with just a touch."

I remove my hand from her dress.

"I'm going to be dripping all day," she huffs.

"Yes, and I'll love it." I lick each of my fingers slowly, torturing both her and myself as I do. *You are doing this for her, to keep her from panicking,* I remind myself as my dick hardens painfully in my jeans.

Fuck, why do I have to be such a martyr sometimes?

I open my door, grab her hand again, and jerk her outside of the car.

She takes a deep breath as she stares up at the massive piece of metal looming over every other boat in the harbor. We can't stand out here for very long. I don't want anyone to spot her that isn't a part of the crew. But I know this is a big moment for her. And I'm not going to take that from her like I've taken everything else.

I hold her against me tightly while my men continue to load up the yacht with supplies.

I don't ask her if she's ready again. She never will be, not truly. It's like jumping into the ocean when you know it's still too cold to swim in, you just have to do it and know you'll survive long enough to find the beauty in it.

I start walking, and she walks with me. There is a ramp, but I'm feeling nostalgic, and I'm hoping it will keep her mind fighting me instead of the trepidation of the boat.

I give her a wink as I release her, and then I jump up onto the main deck. It's a big jump, and the consequences of missing mean I'll take a dip into the ocean water below. But I've done it countless times. I never miss.

I turn to Kai still standing on the deck below. "Your turn," I shout.

It's a risky move. She could take the moment to run away; I already know she doesn't want to do this. But I would chase her down and catch her within seconds.

Her eyes twinkle at the challenge. If we are anything, we are relentless against challenges.

She takes a step back, and I think I was wrong. She's not going to do this. Then she takes a running leap, flying through the air as she sucks all the evil in my life away in a second, before landing firmly on the deck.

She winks back at me. We exchange knowing glances, both remembering the last time we boarded a yacht together all those years ago. And even though it ended in disaster, the moments we stole on that yacht together were something I wouldn't give up for anything.

Our fingers intertwine together as I hear Liesel's voice.

"Am I going to have to pull my luggage up the ramp myself, Black?" Liesel asks.

I smile at her sassiness as I stare down to the deck at her. *She came.* Everyone I care about will be safe. I'll ensure that.

"Zeke and Langston will help you," I say noticing both men hurrying down to collect Liesel's many bags.

I had to practically force Kai to pack an entire bag worth of clothes. She knew we could be gone for months, but she didn't see the need to pack more than a week's worth of clothing. She said she could do laundry. But Liesel, on the other hand, packed her entire life.

It's just another way the two women are so completely different. But they share one thing, I will protect both to the end of my days.

"What is she doing here?" Kai asks.

"Liesel isn't safe from Milo, not after I brought her as my date to his party. I'm making sure everyone on board is safe. Her included," I say.

I feel the tension oozing out of Kai. Her body stiffens, her face pales, and she's no longer thinking about the ache between her legs.

"Are you jealous?" I ask.

"No."

I laugh, because she obviously is.

I lean down and lick around her ear, slowly and seductively. "Don't worry, baby. You are the only one who will be screaming my name later tonight."

I pull away, and her cheeks have flushed as she bites that gorgeous lip I want to taste again.

Mission accomplished.

"Let me introduce you to everyone, and then I'll give you a tour of the boat before we leave." I tighten my grip on her hand as I lead her to where the crew is boarding.

"This is Aidan, the captain. James, Pedro, and Scotty," I say.

"Everyone, this is Kai," I say, not adding her last name. No one needs to know she's a Miller, or pretending to be my spouse, or any other details.

"You will take orders from Kai the same way you would me. She's not just my guest; she's my equal."

Kai smiles at me when I speak. I promised her I'd give her as much freedom as I can while she's still mine, and I plan on keeping my promise.

"And this is my childhood friend, Liesel Dunn. Liesel, this is Kai. I know you two have already met under very different circumstances, but I think you both can become good friends if you want to be."

Liesel holds out her hand to Kai to shake it. Liesel knows exactly what she's doing. She knows Kai doesn't like to be touched.

I frown at Liesel as I pull Kai closer to me, letting Kai know she doesn't need to shake Liesel's hand. She doesn't need to touch anyone while she's here. I will take care of all of Kai's needs.

"Langston can show you which room you'll be staying in, Liesel," I say.

Liesel smiles, cocking her head to the side as she looks to Kai. "We aren't sharing a room? I guess it might get a little crowded if we did."

"Liesel," I threaten with just the one word, and she stops.

Langston scowls at Liesel as well as he grabs her shit and leads her down the where her bedroom is.

I notice Kai out of the corner of my eye giving Liesel a dirty look. And then suddenly, Kai isn't by my side anymore. She grabs Liesel's hat that has blown off her head and races to her.

I should intervene. This could get ugly. Kai will have no

problem punching Liesel, and if Liesel is threatened, she will fight back. These two women have to share the yacht, which is large, but not large enough for these two to never have to interact with each other. But I don't make it in time.

Kai cocks her head at Liesel as she hands the hat to her. "You dropped this. And I wouldn't want you to mistake that I steal things that aren't mine. I don't." Kai's eyes say more. Enzo is mine. And I didn't steal him. He was free for the taking.

That's my girl.

Liesel retaliates by grabbing hold of Kai's hand as she takes the hat back.

Kai just cocks her head and smiles lazily, but I know the touch is killing her. Liesel lets go with a smug smile, but Kai slaps her a little too hard on the back showing she can tolerate touch just fine, especially when she's the one giving it.

"It's good to see you again, Liesel. You look pretty tired though; you should make sure you get some good rest tonight. And make sure Langston doesn't put you in a bedroom near ours. We won't be sleeping much," Kai says, strutting back to me.

Liesel frowns but doesn't say anything as she follows Langston.

"Savage," I say.

Kai shrugs. "Are you ever going to tell me the whole story about Liesel?"

I open my eyes wider. "Do you want me to?"

"Maybe. Not right now."

"Should I give you that tour then?"

She bites her lip again, and I know what she's thinking as her eyelids grow heavy with lust. "Honestly, I just want to explore your body."

I laugh.

"Captain says we are ready to depart," Zeke says interrupting our exchange.

I feel Kai's heartbeat stop next to me. She doesn't breathe; she's a statue next to me.

Don't block this out. Don't block me out.

I pull Kai into me, hoping my arms will warm her enough to bring her back to life.

"Tell him to depart," I say.

Zeke's worried stare moves to Kai. "Is she going to be—"

"She's fine."

Zeke pouts, but does as I say and heads to the bridge to tell the captain it's time for us to leave.

"Kai?"

Nothing.

Fuck.

The tour will have to wait until later. Right now, Kai needs me to bring her back to life. And that's exactly what I plan on doing.

9

KAI

Dammit, the second Zeke mentions we're leaving I close up. It happens automatically, as it almost always does. And then I'm pushing everyone out, Enzo included.

No, no, no!

I'm stronger than this. I fought to be better than this. I'm not going to let this happen—not again.

I am fucking healed.

I will not give in to the fear.

Jarod doesn't get to win.

Milo doesn't get to win.

The memories don't get to win.

I win.

Enzo scoops up my legs in his arms, and I win the first battle of pushing the cold shield down.

"I'm okay," I say.

Enzo smiles, but it's fake. I know he's worried about me. "I know you are. I know you can take care of yourself. You can heal yourself, but this is all my fault. We wouldn't be running if it wasn't for me."

"It is your fault," I say with a teasing smile.

"I know, so let me fix it," his eyes grow dark, and I know what that means. The tour of the yacht will wait till later.

His lips lean down, and he kisses me softly, barely touching me. But it's enough to spark alive the feelings of torture he provoked before. It warms my core and drenches my thighs, all from the lightest touch of his lips.

He's my anchor—the thing keeping me present instead of drifting away into oblivion.

Even when he fucks up, it still makes me want him. It still keeps me anchored to the moment. He keeps me feeling everything.

"You aren't going to give me a tour?" I ask, even though I already know the answer, I just want him to confirm it as he continues to carry me through a door.

"Nope. The only thing I'm giving you a tour of is my body."

I grab his neck and pull his head back down to my face so I can keep kissing him. I don't care if he can't see where he's going while he carries me, I need the distraction.

We stop outside another door.

"You have to stop kissing me for a second, baby," Enzo purrs.

"Why, when you like it so much?" I ask back, still kissing him.

"Because I'll fuck you right here in the hallway if you don't let me open the door."

"You don't need your lips to open the door."

He chuckles as I push my tongue deeper into his mouth.

"Just my eyes," he says, wiggling his eyebrows.

I stop and watch as the system uses facial recognition, a code, and his fingerprint to get through the door.

I must be gaping because Enzo says, "Don't worry, I'll

make sure you know all the codes and the system recognizes you to get to my private bedrooms."

I raise an eyebrow. "Paranoid much?"

"I'm in the security business. Securing yachts is my favorite part. No one will touch you here. Milo will never be able to get to you."

If I was worried before, I'm not now. The way Enzo speaks with such intensity, I know he would take a bullet before he let someone touch me.

"Does every room have this level of security?" I ask.

"No, just yours and mine."

"I like the sound of that."

"The sound of what?"

"You and me."

He grins as he carries me into the room at the end of the hallway. I expected a tiny room with a modest bed; we are after all on a yacht. But this room rivals the one in his beach house mansion.

"Seriously? How is this room so big?"

"The same way everything else about me is big," he wags his eyebrows.

I laugh. I could get used to playful Enzo. I know he's just teasing to keep me distracted from the fact we are now moving. But I could tell the second the engines started. The familiar rock of the yacht starts immediately, and I know it will only get worse the further out to sea we go.

The bed is beautiful, made of light whites and gray linens. I expected it to feel darker in here, but instead, it's heavenly. I remember the cave of a room I stayed in for years; this is the opposite of that. The windows look out into the ocean, but the high ceiling and lights overhead make up for any darkness. I don't feel trapped so much as encased by beauty.

"Put me in the bed and fuck me," I tug on his bottom lip with my teeth.

"No."

I pout. "Why not?"

"Because I want to fuck you against this wall first."

He motions to the almost all glass wall that looks out to the ocean. He flicks a switch, and the wall lights up into beautiful shades of turquoise blue, making the ocean seem illuminated.

"Okay," I bite my lip, liking that idea of being fucked against the wall too much.

He grabs my bare ass under my dress and smirks. "Don't act like you don't like it. You already made it so accessible to reach my favorite parts of you."

His fingers dip between my legs for a split second before retreating back to my ass, leaving me on edge again.

"Enzo, that's not playing fair."

"I never play fair. But then you already know that."

"You're going to kill me tonight."

"And I'm going to love every torturous second of your slow death," he growls.

"Please, I need to come."

He grins. "Do you now?"

"Yes."

He gives me a mischievous grin and then lifts me up until my thighs rest on his shoulders, and my pussy is at his face.

I grab his head. "Oh my god!"

His tongue descends on my already sensitive bud, and I know I'm going to come so fucking hard on his face.

I dig my fingers into his thick hair, holding on tightly as he drives me wild with his tongue, dipping in and out of me before rubbing over my clit.

"Yes, yes, yes!"

He stops.

"Enzo," I growl. I need this. He doesn't get to stop.

I try pressing his head against my pussy, and he chuckles.

"Needy, are we?"

"Yes, please."

He tongue dips in again, swirling, tasting, taunting my lips until I'm going to come and nothing will stop me. He bites down on my clit, and everything stops again.

"No!"

"God, you are so sexy, woman. So goddamn sexy when you are so close and on the edge, but I won't let you come yet. Not until I'm the only thought in your head."

"You are."

He tsks. "I'm not, not yet. You are still thinking about the rocking of the boat. There is still chaos in your eyes. And the second you come, you will start closing the world out again."

"I won't."

"You will."

He licks again, and this time, I let go. I pant. I squirm. I writhe. But I don't shut out the world.

I'm present. I feel the rocking, and instead of shutting it out, I welcome it. I move my hips in rhythm with the boat, putting more pressure on my clit as I ride Enzo's face.

"That's my girl," Enzo moans into my pussy.

"God, I'm so close." And if he prevents me from coming again, it's him I'm going to kill.

"Come, Kai."

I do at the vibration of his words. I explode on his face. My cum is drenching his lips, and my cries are shaking the yacht until I'm sure everyone aboard can hear my screams.

I relax back against the glass wall, unable to catch my breath, and my heart hammering in my chest.

"I'm not done with you yet, beautiful."

"I don't know if I can handle any more. I've never had an orgasm so powerful as that one."

"It's because I denied you so many times. But you are about to have another one."

He slides me down the wall, and I wrap my legs around his waist as he gently tastes my lips.

I taste my cum on his face. I taste too sweet.

"Like how you taste?" he asks.

"Yes."

"Good girl."

He retrieves a condom while holding me up with his other hand. I undo his jeans and push his clothes off as his hard cock springs free, and suddenly I forget about the earth-shattering orgasm I had a moment before. I've never wanted his cock more.

"Hurry," I pant at the sight.

His eyes lust in a deep darkness of want. No man has ever looked at me like Enzo does. Nobody sees me for me. Nobody demands so much from me. Nobody loves me like him.

His sheaths his thick veiny cock with the condom and then thrusts fully into me in one long stroke.

"Fuck!" my nails dig into Enzo's shoulders until I'm sure I'm drawing blood. My mouth devours his as I continue to scream my pleasure into his mouth. My legs squeeze until I'm sure he has trouble breathing.

Enzo doesn't move once he's inside me. He waits for me to adjust to him. Adjust to taking all of him and it never being enough. I want more. I want his cock every damn day.

And I want to be the one that claims the invisible ruthless Black's heart.

"You with me, baby?" he asks.

"Yes, I'm with you. Always."

His tongue slowly traces my swollen bottom lip, teasing me before dipping it into my mouth. I realize he's waiting to see if I'm still fully with him or if I've noticed the rocking of the ship has worsened as we've picked up speed.

"I'm here. I don't care about anything but this."

His eyes move back and forth, searching for the truth.

I smile. "I won't shut you out again. I'm here, truth or lies?"

He smiles. "Fucking truth."

And then he thrusts, fucking me like he's wanted to since we got in his car this morning.

His eyes lock on mine as he thrusts, both of us finding a rhythm together as we move in unison. His eyes tell me everything his mouth never will.

How beautiful he finds me.

How much he likes my fighting spirit.

How much he loves me.

Maybe I'm delusional. Maybe he doesn't love me. Maybe I'm so desperate to feel love I'm imagining it. But when I look into his dark eyes, I no longer see the monster who sold me. I see a broken man who needs saving and healing. I see a man who has dealt with too much pain. And I see a man who loves me.

———

I'VE NEVER SLEPT BETTER.

Never.

It shouldn't be possible for me to sleep so well on a boat,

not after everything horrible in my life has always happened on a ship.

But with Enzo wrapped around my body so tightly, after the most incredible fuck of my life, how could I not sleep well?

Enzo rolls onto his back, and I stare at his naked body. I could get used to this forever. I would even take the running and hiding from our enemies.

This can't last.

Enzo said so himself. We have an expiration date. As soon as the five games are over, then we are over. Black will become the king he was always meant to be and I'll...

I don't know what I'll do. I have no education. No career aspirations. No family. I have nothing. Enzo will ensure I have plenty of money to live off of, I have no doubt about that, but money means nothing.

I need a plan. I need to figure out what I want out of life.

Enzo.

I want Enzo.

But I have to want more than just a man.

Yet the pull is there—I love him. Every second I exist, I realize how stupid I was to not see it before. How he treats everyone else like crap, but me like a princess. How he protects me at the cost of everyone else. He loves me even if he doesn't believe it himself.

I love his sexy grin. I love the ruthless fight in his eyes. I love how we fuck. I love how we fight. I love the chaos that is our life.

And I don't know what to do with that love. If I told him, I think he'd drop me off at the next port. He'd think I'm ridiculous. Maybe I have stockholm syndrome or something. But even though I've been his prisoner, I've rarely felt like I am. He's treated me with more respect than my own father ever did.

My stomach growls, and I see the hint of light shining down through the glass windows, submerged underwater. I don't know how early in the morning it is. But maybe after having a full stomach, I will be able to think more clearly. And bringing Enzo breakfast in bed would be a nice surprise.

I climb out of the bed and find his shirt on the floor. I slip it on and watch as it falls to mid-thigh. I slip my panties on underneath.

Good enough.

I go to the door and open it into the hallway.

I see the main, locked door to Enzo's barracks at the other end only Enzo can use to open this section of the yacht. I open several doors but don't find anything that looks like a kitchen.

I sigh. *I guess I'm going exploring.*

I consider putting more clothes on, but I'm never going to get used to wearing clothes. I'm always going to prefer to be naked as often as I can.

I walk through the door that leads to everyone else on the yacht. It was nice to think Enzo and I were the only ones on the ship for a little while.

But as I walk, I realize the yacht is quiet. All of the bedroom doors are shut. It must be early in the morning still.

I smile, realizing I should be good to sneak up and get food and back down without being detected.

I jog up the stairs and find the kitchen on the main level. The sun is only starting to rise over the horizon. I walk to the large fridge and pull the door open.

"You are up early, stingray. Sleep well?" Zeke asks with a wink.

I close the fridge and walk over to the bar Zeke is sitting at. He takes a pot of coffee and pours me a cup.

"Oh, you prefer your coffee iced, don't you?"

I smile. *How are all of these men not taken?* Zeke shouldn't know how I like my coffee, but he does.

"Hot is fine." I take a seat next to him and cup my hands around the coffee to warm up.

Zeke's eyes cut down and then quickly back up. "Enzo isn't going to like you only wearing his shirt in public."

"Good thing I'm not in public."

Zeke shakes his head. "You are good for him; you know that right, stingray?"

I shrug. "I guess. But I'm also very bad for him."

We sit in silence drinking our coffee.

"What are you doing up so early?" I ask.

"I decided to stay awake after you two decided to keep the entire ship up most of the night."

My cheeks redden, and I gasp. "You heard me?"

"Yep, the walls are usually soundproof enough. But apparently not to contain the cries of a Miller."

"Oh my god! I'm so sorry."

Zeke laughs. "I'm teasing. My bedroom is the closest to yours. It shares a wall. I barely heard you. I'm sure no one else heard you."

I bite my lip. I'm not sure if he's telling me the truth or not.

"But seriously, you can't walk around the ship half naked. Enzo would kill me if he saw me sitting here with you."

I roll my eyes. "Let me handle Enzo."

"I would, but it's my ass he's going to hide for this, not yours."

"You're more of a brother than anything else. Enzo has nothing to worry about."

"He won't see it that way."

I chuckle.

"You love him, don't you?" Zeke asks.

I stop breathing. I didn't realize anyone else could see it.

"Yes," I breathe. It makes it more real, admitting it out loud.

He nods solemnly. "I'm sorry."

"Why are you sorry?"

"Because Enzo will never admit he loves you back. I've seen it happen before. I've seen women spend their lives waiting for Enzo to love them back. He never does. He can't."

"Liesel?" I ask.

He nods. "This won't end in happily ever after."

"I know."

"Enzo doesn't know how to love anyone other than Langston and me. And I'm not even sure if he truly considers us as people he loves or just brothers and that makes it a requirement. Liesel came close, but he doesn't love her. He just protects her. You, you might come the closest to gaining his love. But it's a fight that isn't worth fighting. It will only end in heartbreak for you."

I nod.

"I'm sorry. If he could love anyone, it would be you. You need to finish the game and then leave and forget you ever met any of us."

Leave and forget about the most important man in my life.

Zeke's asking me to leave, rip out my own heart, and tear

it to shreds. Then pretend I didn't just destroy the only meaningful thing that has ever happened to me.

"What if I can't stop loving him?"

"Then you will live the rest of your life in horrible pain. Worse than anything you've ever experienced before. Trust me—find a way to get your heart back before it's too late."

Someone broke Zeke's heart. And he doesn't want to see me get hurt the same way he's constantly hurting. The same way Liesel hurts.

I sigh.

Get my heart back; it should be easy. But I already know it's too late. My heart belongs to Enzo. I stare at my finger where his mother's ring used to sit with the inscription —*My heart belongs to the devil*. The inscription became truth. Was that always going to be my fate from the moment I wore the ring?

I don't know Enzo's mother's entire story, but I do know it didn't end well. The woman fell in love with the devil. The only problem is the devil has no heart to love back with.

10

ENZO

"No! Don't take her!" I yell.

"Kai doesn't belong to you, Enzo. She never did. She doesn't want you. She doesn't like you. She could never love you," Milo says.

I look at Kai smiling in Milo's arms. She leans over and kisses him on the cheek.

I pull out my gun and aim it at them. "Let her go."

"Does she look like a woman that needs to be rescued? She's happy here, with me," Milo says.

"I'll believe it when Kai tells me to leave. That's she's happy here with you."

Milo cocks his head and runs a finger down Kai's neck—my neck. She's mine, not his.

"Beautiful, would you like to tell Enzo how happy you are here with me?" Milo asks.

Kai kisses him softly on the cheek. "Gladly, hubby."

Hubby? They're married?

She looks at me. "I'm happy with Milo. He's the love of my life. He's strong, handsome, and he isn't a monster."

I'm not a monster.

I don't lower the gun, I can't. I don't believe her, or maybe I don't want to believe she could be happy here with him.

Kai is mine.

No, she isn't. She only stayed because you forced her to. You were supposed to set her free. That's how the saying goes. Something like, if you love someone set them free, and if they return they are yours forever.

I could never risk it. I wasn't strong enough to set her free. Because I knew she'd never return to me.

"You're lying. You'll say whatever Milo tells you so he won't kill you," I say.

"Who has the gun pointed at her? It's not me, it's you she fears," Milo says.

I frown. No, she loves me. She wants me.

Milo takes Kai in his arms and forces her to kiss him. He shoves his tongue into her mouth, forcing her to kiss him back. And then she moans, and I lose it.

The gun fires—killing Milo instantly.

And then Kai looks at me, with all of her wrath and I know the truth. She loves him and hates me. I'll never be enough. And I've truly become the monster she thought I was the entire time.

———

I WAKE UP ABRUPTLY. When I sit up, I already know Kai is no longer beside me. I wouldn't have such an evil, cruel dream if she were still near.

I stretch for a second and try to wipe the bad dream from my head.

It was just a dream. It means nothing.

But I know it will stay with me far too long.

I pull on my jeans and a dark T-shirt before I go to find Kai. And I don't even want to know what clothes she put on when she decided to leave my bedroom. Her clothes are still on the floor, and the only thing I notice missing is my shirt from yesterday.

I head to the kitchen first, assuming her stomach decided it needed food and that's exactly where I find her— with Zeke.

I growl when I see him put his hand on her wrist as if to comfort her. But all I see is anger. No one touches Kai without her permission. He knows she doesn't like to be touched, and he did it anyway. It's unacceptable. Especially when she's only half dressed.

I storm toward them and shove Zeke against the wall before either of them hear me.

"What the hell are you doing, touching her?" I scream in his face, huffing out all of my furry into him as I squeeze his neck so tightly he can barely breathe.

"Enzo, let him go! He wasn't doing anything wrong!" Kai yells next to me, trying to pull my hand off of him.

"He touched you for no reason when he knows it hurts you, that's something," I say.

My eyes burn into Zeke's. If he wasn't my brother, I'd throw him overboard for an offense like that. I made a vow to Kai no man would ever hurt her again, and that includes something small like a touch that burns her skin.

"His touch didn't hurt me!" Kai shouts.

"What?"

"His touch doesn't hurt me anymore. At least, it barely registers. And he was just trying to comfort me. Let him go right now," Kai says with her hands on her hips and defiance in her eyes. She will fight me if I don't let him go.

I release my hold. *Damn, that dream fucked with my head and put me on edge more than I thought.*

"Sorry," I say, running my hand through my hair. I walk

over to the pot of coffee, pour myself a cup and down it, needing to walk out of the fog I feel trapped in.

"It's okay, man. I'm going to go check on the captain and see if he needs anything," Zeke says, wisely leaving me alone.

I shake my head, trying to brush off the anger flowing through my veins. I can't. The anger is always a part of me. Always ready to explode at a moment's notice. I used to be better at controlling it, but ever since Kai came into my life, my emotions are all over the place. I'm having feelings I didn't even know existed, and the anger is the hardest to keep in check.

"What the hell was that?" Kai says, shoving me backward.

"You don't want to touch me right now."

"I think I do if you are going to act like an asshole for no reason."

"Just leave it alone, Kai."

"No, I can't. I won't."

"Kai," I warn when she steps so close we are all but touching. "Back up."

I cast my eyes down, keeping the darkness in my gaze away from her.

She stops, and somehow she knows. Her voice grows soft, "What happened?"

My eyes flitter and meet her concerned ones. "Nothing, it was just a dream."

She sucks on her bottom lip, obviously concerned but doesn't ask me any other questions.

I close my eyes, taking a deep breath, and trying to drive my demons out. Her arms slip around me, and instantly, I feel calmer. I know it doesn't hurt her to touch me anymore. It's not a sacrifice. But it still feels that way. No one has ever hugged me in order to comfort me. Not since my mother when I was a young kid.

"Thank you," I breathe out.

"I was trying to bring you breakfast in bed."

"I couldn't stay in bed, not without you. From now on, wake me up first."

She nods against my chest.

"Come on, let me give you the tour I never gave you last night. I know Westcott wants to make breakfast for everyone, and he will be up here soon to make it."

"Okay."

I take her hand again, our fingers intertwining far too naturally. Like a real couple. *We are anything but a real couple*, I remind myself.

I walk her out of the kitchen and onto the main deck. There are several seating areas, strings of lights, and tropical plants that decorate this area. But there is also the looming sea all around us. No walls to hide us from the ocean. There is nowhere for her to pretend we aren't on the ocean. She has to face the water and her own demons.

I suck in a breath waiting for her to shut down or panic because she won't let herself hide away anymore. She doesn't. She slowly walks away from me, trying to drop my hand. At first, I hold her tighter, but I know she needs this. She needs to know she can face it on her own. Especially, if she's going to survive.

So I let go.

Even though it kills me.

Kai takes her time walking to the railing. I keep my feet planted firmly on the ground. I put my hands in my jeans pockets. Let her have this moment alone.

She walks right up to the sea and places her hands on the railing. She closes her eyes and takes a deep breath of the salty air I love and she hates. Her hair blows crazily in the wind, and my shirt rides up her body until I can see her perky ass.

I should make her change, but after seeing her like this, I want her to wear only my shirt the entire trip. I'll just force everyone else to stay in their rooms. *She's fucking breathtaking.*

I give her a few minutes alone, and then I walk up behind her and take her in my arms.

"You are so strong—so much stronger than me. Sometimes I think you would make the better Black," I say.

She leans back into my chest. "You're stronger than you realize."

"Only because of you." I kiss her cheek. "Come on, I have more to show you."

I show her the main deck, the captain's room, and where most of the crew is staying below. I give her the password to my rooms and ensure she knows how to get in. And then I show her the one place I know she will love. The place I know will be a step toward freedom for her. And it terrifies me.

Because I like control. I like that I can make her mine and not worry if she is safe. But I know someday, I have to let her go. I'll probably make Zeke or Langston go with her to protect her. Probably Zeke, she seems to have taken a liking toward him the most.

I take her through my rooms to another door with a similar passcode and eye scan.

"What's this?" she asks. "Another secret room?" her eyes go wide.

"Something like that."

I enter the initial passcode, and then I turn around. "You need to enter a new passcode, one only you know."

"Why?" her voice is so soft as the single syllable leaves her lips.

"Because this room is yours. And yours alone. I don't have the passcode. My face won't work to open the door. It's only yours."

"What?"

"Enter a passcode."

She does, and the door opens. I turn around and push her inside. And then she stares in awe at the room I had Westcott decorate for her. It mirrors mine in many ways but has soft shades of grey and more turquoise that gives it a slightly more feminine feel.

She turns back to me, and I can see water in her eyes.

"There's more than just this room."

"More?"

"Yes, you asked for your freedom. I'm giving you all I can give you."

I walk over to the bed where the electronics and wallet are lying.

"Your phone," I say, handing her a brand new cell phone.

She stares at it like it's a foreign object. But then she never did own a cell phone before to my knowledge. She didn't have the money to own something most people take for granted.

"My number is already programmed into it," I say.

She opens the contacts and smiles. "Giant dick, really?"

I shrug. "I figured it would make you smile."

"And how am I programmed into your phone?"

I wink at her. "Stingray." I took the name Zeke gave to her.

She shakes her head. "You're ridiculous."

"I also got you a laptop in case you decide you need to

start googling porn or something. That's all laptops are good for."

She giggles, running her hand over the shiny metal that's more expensive than the entire trailer she used to live in.

"And these are your credit cards," I say opening the wallet.

"I don't need credit cards. I don't want to spend your money."

"You won't be spending my money; you will be spending your money."

"I don't have any money."

I suck in a breath. Not wanting to say the next words, but knowing I need to. "Yes, you do. I got ten million dollars from Milo...from selling you."

Her face stiffens, and her eyes turn red.

"I know, you will hate me for the rest of your life for that one. And you should. I'm not asking for your forgiveness. I'm saying I don't want the money. I originally was going to use it to give to Rowan to pay for him helping you to escape, but he didn't want the money. The money is yours."

"I don't want the money either."

"It can get you your freedom. You will never have to work. Or you can use the money to do something good, start a business, anything."

She frowns, staring at the wallet.

I'm not going to let her worry about the money. That will be a battle for another day. For now, I just want her to enjoy the little bit of freedom I can give her.

"Come here," I say.

She moves to me silently. And then I press my lips gently to hers.

She smiles against my lips. "You really do want to give me my freedom, don't you?"

"As much as I can." Which I know isn't enough for her. Giving her her own room and phone is nothing. I want her to be free, but I don't know if I could bear it. Even if Milo is dead, letting her go would kill me.

So I don't think about that. I'm done talking.

I grab her hips, sliding my hands up under my shirt she's wearing to feel the curves of her hips as I pull her body tightly against mine. Kai deepens the kiss, pushing her tongue into my mouth as she moans her desire.

I will never get enough of her, and she will never get enough of me.

I hear the knock, but I don't want to acknowledge it. Whoever it is can wait.

Then the doorbell rings, and the video system sounds at Kai's door, indicating someone needs to speak to her.

"Who is that?" Kai asks.

"Ignore it," I say, taking her mouth back in mine. Kai is the only person who matters right now.

The doorbell rings again, and I moan.

"This better be fucking important," I curse as I walk out of Kai's room still gripping her hand to let her know this is not ending. As soon as I deal with whatever asshole problem is behind the door, I will return to fucking her brains out.

She giggles at me as I storm to the door and open it like she can feel all of the rage inside of me.

When I open the door, three pairs of eyes stare back at me.

I frown. "What the hell do you all want?"

Liesel crosses her arms and sways her hips to one side in her bikini top and cover up skirt. "You were the one that dragged me away from my high paying job to sit on a yacht all day. I don't expect to be fucking ignored all trip."

I growl and then turn to Zeke. I raise an eyebrow waiting, but he just glares at Liesel as does Kai next to me. "I was just escorting Miss Dunn to the pool deck."

I turn my attention to Langston. "I have news from Rowan about Milo Wallace," Langston says.

I crack my knuckles trying to remain calm. I need to get everyone off this fucking boat if for no other reason than for them to stop driving me nuts. If I could just have Kai and myself on this yacht by ourselves I would. For a second I consider moving them all to a second yacht so Kai and I can fuck in complete privacy, but I know it's better for her protection if my best men are here.

"Zeke, continue the task at hand," I say.

"My pleasure," Zeke says, winking at Kai as he lifts Liesel over his shoulder.

"Put me down, you brute," Liesel shouts.

Kai tries to contain a snicker next to me, but it still escapes.

I sigh, running my fingers through my hair. I wish Kai and Liesel could get along. It would be better for everyone, but Liesel doesn't play nice with anyone. She never has. And Kai doesn't understand Liesel and my's past.

Now that I have gotten rid of Liesel and Zeke, I turn my attention to Langston. I want to order him to leave, but I need to hear what news he has about Milo.

"Speak," I order, running out of patience.

"Milo has returned to Italy. He's injured, as are a few of his best men, but they will all make a speedy recovery. He's pissed, obviously, but assumes Rowan stole Kai from him. Rowan is doing some reconnaissance and thinks the best time to attack Milo is when he's on his yacht, not at his home."

I frown, not sure about that. Milo bought one of my yachts; I know its capabilities. But I prefer to attack at sea, and it seems Rowan feels the same.

"I want you to get me the full blueprints of both Milo's home and his yacht. I want to know everything about both locations and have our own plan of attack. Tell Rowan we will be speaking soon; I will not let Milo continue to live and put Kai at risk. I want him dead."

Kai shudders next to me at the mention of Milo's name. I want Milo dead now. I won't let him come near Kai again. I want to protect my men from this dangerous asshole, but with Rowan's team on our side, we have twice the army Milo does. Milo's days are limited. I will kill him. I will set Kai free from any man who tries to claim her, including myself.

11

KAI

Enzo wants Milo dead.

I'm surprised he's had as much self-control as he's had. I figured now that he has me trapped on a yacht with his best men, he would have gone on a mission by himself to take out Milo. It's only a matter of time until Enzo gets impatient waiting.

Enzo is smart. He's ruthless. He can be patient. But not when it comes to me. He wants me safe, yesterday.

And when he goes to kill Milo, he will go alone. He won't risk his men. He won't start a war with a man as dangerous as Milo over something personal.

Rowan may want revenge, but Enzo needs to heal the hurt he feels for betraying me. Enzo will never forgive himself for what he did. Even after I do. Even after he kills Milo.

And I'm terrified of what will happen when Enzo goes for Milo. Enzo is powerful, dangerous, and strong. I've never seen him fail in hand to hand combat. But Milo won't play fair. I know that from my limited time with Milo. He's cruel in a way that Enzo never will be. Enzo's father may have trained him to be cruel, but deep down that's not who Enzo is. Enzo is fair, ruthless, and he demands loyalty above everything else. But he would never kill or torture just for the sake of killing. He would never kill for his own amusement.

Milo does. He kills because he enjoys killing.

That's why Milo has made so many enemies. That's why Rowan hates Milo as much as Enzo does. I don't know who Rowan lost to Milo, but I know he did. I could see it in Rowan's eyes when he stole me from Milo. He's felt pain I can only imagine. I've felt plenty of physical pain, but nothing like what Rowan has felt.

His pain is different. His pain rocks you to the core and lives inside in a cage that digs deep into his heart, tearing away at it slowly until there is nothing left. He lives with the loss of someone he loved every single day.

While I only live with the scars of what happened to me.

My eyes drift to Enzo still gripping my hand. A second ago, I was prepared to fight Liesel; my jealousy had gotten the better of me. I wanted to rip out her throat for thinking Enzo could ever be hers. But now I realize how stupid I was being. I would gladly let Liesel have Enzo if it meant he was safe.

Because right now, I fear for his safety. I don't know if he will survive a battle with Milo. And that pain would destroy me.

I need more answers. I need a way to protect Enzo while also defeating Milo. Rowan might be that answer, but I don't trust a man I hardly know. I don't trust anyone. Not even my own father.

My father.

He's betrayed me more than any man ever has. Because even though Enzo sold me to Milo, Enzo also saved me.

My father sold me and then never came for me. He didn't rescue me. He didn't save me.

And the only way I can truly heal is by facing him. By figuring out why and maybe learning more about this stupid game that hold Enzo and I captive. We're slaves to such a stupid game, all for a chance at ruling an empire I don't want. And one Enzo suffers too much for. Because I know if one of his men were under attack, if one of his men's wives were stolen by Milo like I was, he would still do everything fucking possible to get them back and make Milo pay.

"I need to talk to my father," I say, seemingly out of nowhere. Two seconds ago, we were talking about Rowan and Milo; my father didn't even enter the equation. But for all I know, my father was the one who sent Milo. He was the one to set the trap Enzo fell for when he sold me.

Langston takes a step back as if he knows he shouldn't be involved in such a personal conversation, but I don't care. Langston is more family to me than my father will ever be.

Enzo studies me for less than a second, not at all surprised by my change in topic. He's been waiting for me to bring up my father this entire time.

Enzo nods and then turns to Langston. "Arrange for Mr. Miller to meet us at a set location. I don't want him to know he is meeting us. Just give him an order through the usual chain of command."

"Yes, sir," Langston says, disappearing and leaving Enzo and I alone again—at least until Liesel escapes Zeke's grasps and comes begging for attention again. I know I need to talk to Liesel and make things civil between us. I don't know her whole story, but I know her story is important if she was let into Enzo's deepest circle. But I'll face Liesel later.

I should want to jump back into Enzo's arms and fuck him like we were planning to moments before. He gave me everything he could, inching me closer to my freedom, and I've never felt closer to him. But right now we are both too on edge to fuck.

All I want is to cuddle in Enzo's arms while I plan what I'm going to do with my father. I want to hold Enzo close to me for as long as possible, because I don't know how long I have left with him. Whether Milo kills him or Enzo finally sets me free, one way or another—our story ends the same, with my heartbreak.

Enzo squeezes me close to him, and I already feel my heart breaking. *I'm such a goner.*

12

ENZO

I STEP foot onto the Raptor, the yacht of mine Mr. Miller captains, with all of my furry flowing through me with a force I haven't felt since I screwed up and sold Kai to Milo. It is going to take everything inside me not to kill this bastard the second I see him. He's the reason Kai was tortured for six years. He is the reason she came back to try and claim the Black empire instead of staying gone. He is the reason I ended up hurting her.

No, I take responsibility for my own actions. I hurt her. I won't let Mr. Miller take any of the blame.

But I am going to make him pay for what he did to Kai. I will pay every day of my life with every breath. I vowed to protect her with more than my life. And I plan on living that way.

Miller will eventually pay with his life, but not before Kai orders me to kill him. She will; she's as ruthless as I am deep down. But I'm not sure she's ready to kill her own father. That's the kind of thing that takes years of abuse to develop. It needs to be personal. It needs to consume your every thought and every nightmare. Only then does someone turn to something as extreme as killing your own father. I should know.

I walk slowly and deliberately to the main office on the yacht in the middle of the night. A few crew members notice me, but they know better than to ask me any questions. I take a seat in the office like I own the place, and I do. I haven't stepped foot on this particular yacht in years—mainly because of fucking Miller. I never trusted him, not when I knew he was Kai's father. Not when I found out he never searched for her when she went missing. Not when I discovered he lived in a trailer for a house instead of a mansion. I pay him well enough to afford much more. And the story he's fed Kai over the years about his wife's hospital bills taking all his money is bullshit.

And all my suspicions were proved correct when I found out he was the one who sold Kai.

I wait for Mr. Miller, but I won't wait for long. I'm giving him five minutes to get his ass into this office before I come after him and shoot him in the leg for making me wait. Kai can't fault me too much for shooting him. Not when she experienced worse for years.

The door opens and Mr. Miller steps inside, his head up and proud, staring down at me like I'm vermin instead of a king. He stares down at me like I am less than, instead of worthy of all his attention. I guess I should thank him for passing the trait onto his daughter, because I love that she is the only woman who has ever truly stood up to me.

"You summoned me," he says, not taking a seat in the chair opposite me.

"Sit," I command.

He hesitates.

"Sit, or I'll make you sit."

He huffs like he knows I won't.

Try me, old man.

When he sits, I notice the wrinkles around his eyes have deepened, the gray in his hair now covers his entire head of hair, even down to his beard. He truly looks like an old man. His muscles have weakened through the years. If he were any other of my men, I would retire him or fire him depending on how loyal he'd been to me over the years. But I can't do either without pissing off Kai and breaking the rules since I'm required to run everything by her as co-Black for now.

I shouldn't even be having this meeting without informing her. But this conversation will stay between us. This conversation will not leave this room.

Mr. Miller folds his hands in his lap while he spreads his legs, taking up the entire chair. He seems relaxed, but I can read people easily. He's not relaxed. He knows I could end him as easily as I snap my fingers. He's afraid of me.

"Why?" My entire body goes into that one word. One question has never been this important.

He laughs like I asked the most ridiculous question. "That's not the question you should be asking. You already know why I sold her."

I growl. He's not even going to apologize for what he did. He made the decision as easily as he decided his breakfast this morning.

"It's the question that matters to me. You hurt her. You answer to me."

He chuckles again. "Why? Because you love her? You don't care about my daughter any more than I do. Rumor is you sold her to our enemies. You don't give a fuck, so stop pretending you do. If you need to take out your vengeance on someone, fine, take it out on me. But don't act like you are any better than me."

I storm toward him and kick him hard to the floor; he falls off balance and slams into the floor beneath him. My boot lands on his chest, pressing hard enough I know it's hard for him to breathe.

"You will tell me everything. Or I will kill you."

He spits at me. "I will tell you nothing more than what you deserve. And you don't deserve the truth. You already know why I sold her, the same reason your father tortured you night after night. To toughen you up in order to win the empire."

My eyes grow wide with anger. "And you know how I felt about my own father."

He snickers using too much of his air as he does. "You fucking slaughtered him."

"What makes you think I won't do the same thing to you?"

"Because as much as you pretend to be cruel, you aren't. You didn't actually sell my daughter, and you are too much of a pussy to hurt her."

I press my foot into his neck, shutting him up, but I'm careful not to leave any visible markings. I don't want Kai to know I roughed up her father before I let her meet him.

I study him and realize he's bluffing. He knows nothing about the game. He didn't trick me into selling Kai to Milo. He's not working with Milo. He knows nothing. He's just pretending to know something in order to stay alive.

Fucking pussy.

"Listen to me. If it were up to me, I'd kill you right here on the floor of this grungy office and never think about you again. But it's not up to me. You're Kai's father. And I know the decision has to be hers."

He tries to speak, but I dig my boot in deeper.

Self-control. Keep it together. Don't give into the anger.

"This is how it's going to go. At dawn, Kai and I are going to board this yacht so she can get her questions answered. You will not let her know you and I spoke. You will answer all of her questions, honestly. You will apologize for everything bad you have ever done to her. You will be a father. You will promise to protect her from now on and never hurt her again. And you will promise to stay out of her fucking life. Do you understand?"

I ease my foot from his throat.

He coughs.

"Or what? You'll kill me? You already told me you wouldn't do that for Kai's sake."

My face reddens as the anger explodes through my body. "I will kill you if you don't do as I command. I've fucked up plenty of times where Kai is concerned. I'll deal with her wrath if I have to. But I vowed to not let any man hurt her ever again. That includes you."

He scowls. "You wouldn't. You are too much of a pansy."

I shrug. "Maybe. Maybe I wouldn't kill you." I press my boot harder into his throat, no longer caring that it will leave a mark. I watch his face turn purple and blue from lack of oxygen. And then I lean down close like I'm telling him a fucking secret.

"But there are worse things than death. Just ask your daughter about that."

I release him and watch as the bastard wiggles on the floor, begging for oxygen. I only gave him a few seconds of what he put his daughter through and he could barely handle it—*the coward.*

I walk to the door, ready to return to Kai who I had to leave sleeping naked in my bed to come talk to this asshole.

"You think you got everything figured out," Mr. Miller says.

I turn as I reach the door. "I do."

He shakes his head. "You don't know nothing. You don't know the fucking truth. You don't know the pain coming both of your ways. There is so much you don't know, boy."

Old feelings stir when he calls me, boy. The only other person that ever called me, boy, was my father. And I hated him for it.

I slam my fist into his face, watching the blood spurt from his nose as I do. So much for not letting Kai know I was here. She'll know the second she takes a look at her father. But I'm done hiding secrets from her, and I don't regret one second of my time with her father.

13

KAI

"ARE YOU READY?" Enzo asks me, as I roll up my sleeves on the buttoned-down shirt I decided to wear.

I wanted something that made me feel powerful, as an equal to my father and Enzo, but I'm not sure it mattered what I wear. I have huge butterflies bouncing around in my stomach.

How can I ever be ready to face a father who sold me?

I nod when I finish rolling my sleeves up, revealing enough of my scars, but not too much.

I want answers.

I want an apology.

I don't want to show him the pain I experienced. He doesn't deserve my pain.

Enzo holds out his hand instead of taking mine like he usually does. He's going to let be the one in control today. If I don't want Enzo with me, all I would have to do is ask him to leave. He'll be right by my side if I want him to, or he'll remain only as a guard protecting me but not interfering.

I want to face my father on my own. But I could use Enzo's help getting to that point.

I take his hand that instantly warms me.

We walk up the decks of the yacht and meet Langston and Zeke on the top deck. Both of them are solemn in their dark jeans and black T-shirts. They look like they are about to do battle. And I have no doubt they know as much as I do about my father, possibly more.

I notice the other yacht anchored next to us and the ramp that leads from ours to theirs that Langston and Zeke have been guarding.

Enzo gives them a nod, and they silently traipse across the ramp. Enzo and I follow with my hand still gripped in his. When we reach the yacht my father captains, all the men stop as if we are royalty. They practically bow at us as we walk.

I don't feel like a scared little girl anymore. I feel like a woman about to deliver her vengeance.

We reach a door, and our group stops. Langston and Zeke face away like they are ready to jump in front of a bullet to protect me. All the men on this yacht work for Enzo, so I don't know what we have to fear here. I think they are more likely here to intimidate my father.

"Your father will meet you here," Enzo says hesitating outside the door waiting for me to invite him in. But he already knows I won't. I need to face my father on my own. Enzo doesn't protest or ask to enter with me.

He leans down and kisses me on the cheek. "You got this." He doesn't say he'll be here if I need him. The confidence in his voice tells me he doesn't think I will need him.

I open the door and leave the only men who care about me outside while I enter the room where I'll face my father.

The lock of the door behind me sounds like a closing to my soul. I'm trapped in this room that smells like blood and musk and men. A room my father and the rest of his crew enter to handle business and probably beat the shit out of each other when one of them fucks up.

I take a deep breath in and out, filling my lungs to prepare to speak to my father. My neck still throbs, but my voice is easier to use now. I don't even have to wear the gauze covering anymore, but the stitches are starting to itch like a motherfucker.

There is a large oak desk with an executive chair I know I'm supposed to sit behind. It would give me control over the situation. Sitting behind that desk would make it clear I'm the boss and my father is nothing but a peon who needs to follow my orders.

But he's still my father, and I don't want to face him with a desk between us. So I pull the two chairs on the opposite side of the desk apart until they are facing each other and take a seat in one and wait.

My stomach does flips while I wait, which isn't long. The door opens, and my father is standing in the doorway only minutes later. His face is bruised, and there is dried blood on his nose and the collar of his shirt. His hair looks disheveled, and his neck is heavily bruised.

He looks like he got in a fight mere hours ago. I notice Enzo standing behind him, staring at him with intense disgust. Like he wants to put a bullet between his eyes, instead of letting him into this office.

My eyes return to my father. Enzo did this. It has his mark all over him. He met with my father before he let me speak with him.

I should be angry at Enzo for controlling my life, but I'm not. I'm grateful. My father deserves every bit of pain he's in and more, and I'm not strong enough to deliver the same level of punches Enzo can.

"Take a seat," I command, not getting up from my own chair.

My father stiffens before the door is closed behind him. Then he takes a seat opposite me, crossing his legs like we are meeting for a casual lunch instead of meeting to discuss why he sold me.

He folds his hands in his lap, and for the first time, I realize how old he looks. He's in his late sixties and still working, but I doubt he can handle the physical nature of this job much longer.

Questions fill my head—so many questions. But I don't ask them. I let the silence fill the room, letting the silence stretch and unnerve him.

"What are you doing?" he asks.

I cut my eyes to him. "Thinking of all the ways I could kill you."

"You wouldn't kill your own father."

"Maybe not, but I'm not sure I consider you a father anymore. Fathers don't sell their daughters. Fathers don't lie to their daughters their entire lives."

"That's what you are pissed at? That I didn't tell you about the stupid game? The empire you could inherit if only you were strong enough?"

"No, I'm pissed I thought I grew up with a father mourning the loss of my mother, doing everything he could to survive, and instead, I was raised by an evil sack of shit who didn't prepare me for my own future."

"Ask your fucking questions, I have work I need to get back to."

I lean forward, putting all my anger into my stare. I consider sitting in silence so I can piss him off further, but I can't stand to be in this room with him any longer than I have to.

"My mother's hospital bills, are you really in such debt that you can't afford a house bigger than that trailer?"

"No."

Fuck, this is going to gut me.

"Then, why did we live in a trailer?"

"Because I wanted to toughen you up. I didn't want you to become a princess like how Enzo was raised. You learned how to handle yourself in that trailer."

I close my eyes, willing myself to ask the next question.

"Did mom really die from cancer?"

"No, your mother was an alcoholic. She drank too much and killed herself."

My mouth falls open as my heart breaks. I don't remember my mother. All I know is the story. She fought so hard to stay alive for me that we incurred an incredible debt we could never repay. It was a lie. All of it. *A fucking lie!*

But then every word out of my father's mouth is a lie.

And it doesn't shock me that my mother didn't care about living for me either.

I want to get out of here. I want to get back to the Savage with Enzo and pretend I'm an orphan, that my father died along with my mother back then. But I have one more question I need to ask. A question I already know the answer to, but I have to ask it. I need to hear it from his lips.

"Why did you sell me?"

His eyes look into my soul, and I know it's not out of love or compassion or sorrow for what he did to me. He doesn't tear up thinking about it. He doesn't regret putting me through the pain.

He hurt me because he wanted me to be stronger. He hurt me because he thought I was too weak to win without experiencing pain.

"I sold you so you would have a chance to win. I did it for you."

"No!"

My single word vibrates through the room until it consumes both of us.

"No, you didn't sell me so I had a chance to win. You sold me because you are evil and cruel. You sold me so if I were to win, I could give you a better life. Promote you in the ranks, and the Miller line would continue on ruling for another generation. You didn't do this for me. You did this to me. You hurt me. Broke me. Caused me more pain than my body could physically handle, until I learned to shut it out."

I think back to Enzo's father. I don't know what he did to prepare Enzo to become Black, but I know it wasn't kind. It was personal and dark and cruel. But at least he was a father. At least he didn't pretend to be something he wasn't and hide behind a lie. He spoke the truth to his son and showed him his darkest side, while my father pretended all this time.

"You are nothing but a coward. There were other ways to prepare me that didn't involve selling me. Teaching me how to wield a gun and weapons. Teaching me how to fight. Educating me on how this business runs. Preparing me for every scenario. You didn't have to sell me!"

A sob escapes my throat, and I curse myself for showing weakness to this man.

"Are you finished?" he asks.

I grit my teeth together to keep from launching myself at him. "No. You haven't even apologized for what you did."

"And I'm not going to. You had to be sold."

"Why? Why was that the only way your twisted little brain could think to prepare me?"

He leans forward, glaring right back at me. His nostrils flare, and his anger spreads from his face to his bones.

"I've been in this world a lot longer than you, Katherine. You don't understand the dangers you will face. You don't understand how strong you have to be to become Black."

"One, don't call me Katherine. My name is Kai."

He shakes his head.

"And two, you don't understand the strength required to be Black. You failed, remember? Enzo's father won, not you. You have no right to think you know better than me the strength it takes."

My father sighs, falling back in his chair in defeat.

I win.

But it doesn't feel like a win. It feels like pain.

"I don't want to ever see you again," I say.

"Fine, then stop summoning me and I'll never see you again."

It's not enough. I want him out of my life forever. I consider going outside and retrieving Enzo's gun, but then I think better. That's not who I am. I'm not cruel. I will not kill my father.

"I want you to leave Miami. I want you to move to California or Canada or Belize or Ireland. Anywhere that's hundreds of miles from me. Anywhere not connected to the sea or Miami."

He cocks his head. "I can't exactly leave Miami or the sea when I'm a captain."

"You aren't a captain anymore. You're fired."

That gets his attention. His face goes pale. "You can't fire me."

I cock my head to the side. "Did you forget the rules you helped to create? While the games are being played, Enzo and I have equal control of the company. And I'm currently in the lead one to nothing. So I have plenty of power. And I'm firing your ass, effective immediately. This ship's next mission will be to get your ass to the farthest away land, away from me."

"You can't fire me," he whispers like I just ripped out his heart.

"I just did."

I stand, effectively dismissing him. I never plan on seeing my father ever again. It's not the same as killing or punishing him for what he did to me, but it's enough.

He stands too, facing me. And I can tell he has more to say, but it's too late for an apology. I won't change my mind about firing him.

I walk to the door and open it. Enzo's eyes meet mine, searching to see how much pain I'm in, but the pain is gone. My father no longer exists to me.

Enzo smirks when he reads my face.

"My father is fired. Tell the men they are to drop him off at port as far away from here as possible and to promote the second in command."

Enzo raises an eyebrow.

I step closer to him and whisper so only he can hear. "And if you have a problem with me ordering that without discussing with you first, we can have a discussion about you meeting with my father first and beating the shit out of him."

"I don't have a problem with you making the decision. It's yours to make."

I nod. "And thank you for beating the shit out of my father. He deserved every punch."

He grins.

My father walks to the door where I'm standing. He glares at Enzo like he's the devil. He is, but he's my devil.

The kind I can trust to protect me. The kind who fucks up and then makes up for it. Not the kind that sells me and pretends that is somehow saving me.

My father leans over to me, alcohol heavy on his breath as he says, "There is so much more you don't know, Kather —Kai. So much more. Find the truth before Enzo does. It's the only way to win."

I straighten and look my father dead in the face and speak loud enough so everyone can hear my declaration. "I don't want to win."

14

ENZO

WE RETURN across the plank to our ship in silence. I hold out my hand to her as I did before. Walking onto the ship, she held my hand like we were a team. Walking off, she didn't take my hand.

I don't know what her father said to her, but it wasn't an apology. It wasn't what I told him to say.

She fired him. That was her vengeance. She's hoping by sending him away she will be able to heal and get over this. She doesn't realize a child never gets over the betrayal of their own father.

Never.

It's something I will live with the rest of my life.

And so will she.

Kai walks straight for our private rooms once aboard our yacht. She is in no mood to talk or be around other people. I unlock the doors for her because it will be faster than waiting for her to do it herself. I hold the door open, and she steps inside. She heads directly toward her room.

She hasn't slept in that room since she boarded the yacht. She's stayed in my room, but right now, it looks like she wants to be alone. And I can't handle that. I want to help her. I want to heal her. And I can't do that if she locks me out.

I put my hand on the door to her room, stopping her from opening it.

"Want to get a drink with me before bed?"

She looks at me, and I see the pain etched on her face. I want to make her smile. I want her to be happy. But she can never be happy here with me. She will never be happy until she is free of this life.

She takes a deep breath, probably to tell me off.

"We can play a game while we get a drink," I say, hoping that getting to play a game of truth or lies with me will sweeten the deal.

She smiles softly. "Okay."

It's the most beautiful word I've heard. It warms me to know I get to spend a few more hours with her. Even if she doesn't share my bed tonight, I will still have this.

I don't hold out my hand to her again; I already know she won't take it. I think she thinks that by not touching me she will break our connection, that I won't be able to read her mind as easily if I can't feel her.

But I don't need to touch her to understand her. I feel her heart fluttering too quickly in her chest. I feel the throbbing ache in her chest. I feel the coolness of her breath. She wants to shut down so she doesn't feel. That's why she wanted to go back to her room alone. So she could go back to her icy cage and not feel anything.

I open the door to the lounge, decorated with beautiful, elegant white couches and soft lights to make it feel light and airy. There is an all-glass bar in the corner, and the room could easily fit fifty people for a party. Instead, it usually only holds me, and now Kai. I don't need more than that.

"What do you want to drink?" I ask as I walk behind the bar.

She stares at all of the high priced liquors floating on a glass shelf overhead.

The yacht rocks hard, and we both grip onto the cool glass of the bar to keep from falling over. My eyes lock with hers trying to calm her, but I don't see as much fear as I would expect. Her father hurt her too much to care about a rocking ship at the moment.

It rocks again, and I know we are heading into treacherous waters. Storms are coming, both natural and man-made. Milo will be coming soon if we don't attack first. And we still have to face the second round of games.

Kai steadies herself and grins as she stares up at a bottle of liquor. A cheap bottle. I don't even know how it got onto this yacht.

"No," I say.

"Yes," she says.

"No way. We are not drinking that poison."

She nods hungrily. "Yes, we are. If you don't want me to head to my room right now and shut everything out, then you are drinking with me, and I get to choose the drinks. And I choose shots of Jagermeister."

"Ugh," I moan. "I don't think my stomach can handle it."

"Come on, Black. I thought you were made of stronger stuff."

She's back to calling me Black again. And I didn't miss her declaration to her father. She doesn't want to be Black. She just wants this to be over. She wants to pretend this life never existed. *That I never existed.*

It hurts, but not as much as drinking this liquor is going to.

"Fine."

She smiles triumphantly and climbs up on the counter to reach the bottle herself.

I reach for a couple of high ball glasses so I can at least mix coke or something into it to disguise the taste.

She wags her finger at me. And then reaches behind me for the shot glasses.

Oh, hell no.

"Seriously? Shots?"

She nods. "We are about to get wasted."

I sigh. I would do anything for this girl. She has somehow snuck onto my very limited list of people I would lay down my life to protect. That list includes Langston and Zeke. Both brothers who would protect me as readily as I protect them. Then there is Liesel and Kai. Only four people I truly care about.

Kai carries the bottle and shot glasses over to the biggest couch, sits, and pours two shots.

I sit next to her and reluctantly take one of the glasses. She holds hers out with a huge smile on her face, and suddenly this is all worth it. I'd drink myself to death with the shitty liquor just to see her smile.

We both slam the drink down, and I try not to vomit from the taste.

"Why do you like this so much?"

"I grew up on this shit. You think my father could afford better?"

Yes, I think your father could afford a lot more on the quarter of a million dollar salary we paid him each year.

She frowns, realizing her mistake, and pours another shot for each of us.

"So what do you think the next round in the game will be?" she asks, trying to move on from her father.

I sigh. "I don't know. But if I know my father, it will be cruel and twisted. Something neither of us wants to do."

Her eyes grow bigger at that thought. Stealing from Milo was easy. He was a rich asshole who stole and beat women. He deserved everything and more than we did to him. But my dad could order us to kill an innocent. And at least one of us would have to do it if we want the games to stop.

She raises the new shot. "To shitty fathers."

"To shitty fathers."

We both down another shot of poison. This time it goes down a little easier.

"You start," she says, referring to the game of truth or lies I promised. She pours more liquor into both of our glasses while I lean back, getting comfortable on the couch.

I say the first thing I'm thinking, "I healed after what my father did to me, and so will you. Truth or lie?"

"Lie, drink," she says. She downs her shot, and so do I. She refills our glasses before she speaks.

"I forgave my father for selling me."

"Lie," I say as we both slam another drink down.

Kai wasn't kidding about getting drunk. With the number of shots we are drinking, we are going to be completely hammered.

The ship heaves again—and maybe that's a good thing. She will pass out and be able to sleep through the storm.

"I forgave myself for selling you."

She frowns like my lie is painful to her. It shouldn't be. She will never forgive me, and I will never be able to either.

"Lie," she says quietly. We both drink, but it's more somber this time.

She bites her lip, considering her next truth or lie.

"I could never forgive you," she says.

"Truth," I sigh, knowing it's true.

She shakes her head. "I already forgave you."

My pupils dilate, and my heart races as if she admitted her deepest secret. She didn't, but the emotions that spill from her words consume me. *How can she forgive me?* She's lying—to me or to herself.

What I did was unforgivable. But we are both too drunk for me to argue with her about it now. So I keep playing the game instead.

If she wants to get deep, then so will I.

"I killed my father," I say, admitting something I've never said to anyone.

Kai looks at the scars she can see on my hands. She looks at the pain in my eyes and the fire in my soul. She's seen how black my heart can get. I've never told her any stories about how my father trained me. I've never told her stories about how cruel my father could be. But she knows. She sees the evidence on my skin and heart.

She didn't kill her father for what he did to her. But I did mine. And she will probably hate me for stooping to his level.

"Good, he deserved to die. Did you make him suffer?"

"Yes, when I became stronger than him, I snuck into his office. I made him bleed on every surface of the office he loved and then painted the walls with his blood. Only when he showed how weak he could be, did I kill him."

She licks her lips like what I just said turned her on.

I shake my head. *We are two messed up motherfuckers.*

The boat rocks and I wince, preparing for the fear and pain on her face. She downs her last shot.

"I'm not afraid of the water anymore. The rocking

doesn't scare me. Not when there is something so much more treacherous I fear."

Milo?

Does Milo now consume all her thoughts that she no longer has more than one fear?

I don't get to tell her I think it's a truth. I don't get to ask her what she's terrified of. Because she launches herself on top of me, her lips meeting mine as her hips grind onto my crotch.

We've both drank so much our bodies literally shouldn't be able to fuck at our level of intoxication. But with one kiss I sober up quickly, and my cock hardens into stone.

Her tongue dips into my mouth as if she's been doing it for years, and I'm the liquid she yearns to taste, not the liquor. She tastes like cheap alcohol. It should turn me off; instead, it makes me crave more.

Shit, now I'm going to want to drink Jager all the time because it reminds me of her.

I slip my hand under her shirt, letting her cool skin ease my senses. The self-control it takes to keep the devil inside instantly takes over when I touch her. Her skin makes me feel human in a way I haven't felt since I was a young kid.

She makes me think I'm not a monster. But I'm just fooling myself. She only pushes the monster away for a few minutes while I focus on her.

I reach for her pants, and she swats my hand away.

"Just kiss me and hump me like two teenagers making out on their parents' couch. Only when you can't help but not have me do I want you to fuck me."

Jesus.

I'm already there, but I don't tell her that. I flip us over and do exactly what she asks. She wants to get a teenage experience she never had, fine. But after that, she is going to get all man.

I drive my hips into her spread legs, letting her feel as much as she can through our clothes as I dip my tongue in and out of her mouth, kissing her like she's never been kissed before.

My kisses should be messy and drunk, but they've never been so focused on my mission of getting Kai to beg for me to strip her naked and fuck her with my fingers, tongue, and cock.

I want it all tonight.

She didn't tell me what she fears yet, but I want to take it all away. I will drive it away with sex—at least for tonight. And tomorrow, I'll figure out what looms over her.

I grind my cock again into her core as her body grips my waist with her legs, begging for so much more than she will ever admit to me.

What are you hiding, pretty girl?

I want to fuck it out of her, but that's not fair. She told me her truth during the game. Now I just have to figure out my own truth.

I don't know how teenagers make out on the couch anymore. That was something I was never privileged enough to experience. Not because I didn't have women lining up for me at that age, but because my youth was stolen too soon. At that age, I was treated like a man. My fucks were with women, not teenaged girls.

"Are you okay?" Kai asks, stopping our kisses and looking into my eyes like she can see what haunts me.

I smirk. "Yes, I'm about to fuck the most beautiful woman in the world."

She cocks her head. "You already decided you are going

to get lucky, huh? You still have to win me over, convince me to fuck you."

I nuzzle her neck and kiss the tender spot there. "I already have."

I want to torture her slowly, but I have no patience or self control when it comes to her. She controls my body and soul. I've never been in a more dangerous position than when I'm with her.

"Fuck me, Black."

One command and I yield to her.

I could never deny her.

Before this is all over I'm going to sacrifice everything for this woman, I can feel it deep down to my bones.

I pull her pants down before sliding my own down. I barely have time to sheath myself with a condom before my cock grows a mind of its own and slides into her slick pussy.

She groans, and I lose my shit.

Why does making her feel good drive my every action?

Why does she have this hold over me?

I thrust, feeling her tightness and enjoying the beautiful glaze of her eyes as she releases whatever fear she's dreading.

What is it about Kai that makes everything different?

She has a pussy and a tight body like every other woman I've been with. She's beautiful and smart and fearless, but there are plenty of women in the world with similar attributes.

Is it because we share similar life experiences? Both raised by fathers more concerned with winning an empire than raising children? Both spending our entire adult lives fighting for something we don't really want?

That's part of it, but there is something deeper I don't

understand. And when my cock is inside her, like it is now, I have no hope of figuring it out.

I watch her mouth change into a beautiful O shape as she cries out her orgasm. With every other woman, I make her come because it stokes my ego. It makes me feel godlike to know I can control something so intimate. With Kai, simply seeing her orgasm brings me as much pleasure as my own.

Her body settles down, her orgasm finishing its course, and I'm frozen. I just awe in the beauty on her face.

"Enzo? What are you doing?" Kai asks bashfully.

"Watching you."

She bites her gorgeous lip.

"Aren't you going to come?"

"Yes, but I didn't want to ruin this moment. I wanted to be able to watch every second of your orgasm."

"I'm done now."

I laugh. "You aren't anywhere close to done."

I pound into her body and watch as her body responds. And I know I'll pull another orgasm out of her soon.

This woman.

This beautiful, broken woman is going to be the end of me.

She is going to take everything.

My house.

My money.

My men.

My family.

My empire.

It will all be hers by the end. I don't want the empire any more. It means nothing if I can't keep her safe. I don't care about winning; I only care about protecting her.

Tomorrow I'll do more surveillance of Milo Wallace.

He's her biggest threat at the moment. He's my new mission. Killing him, and then sending a message to the world that Kai Miller is never to be touched.

Kai may never belong to me, but she doesn't belong to them either.

She's like the wild ocean waves, uncontrollable and with the power to take over the world with one crash if she wanted to. Her wrath will eventually decimate me in one mighty hurricane. Because that is who she is. She can pretend she forgives me, but deep down, she will never let that pain go until she destroys me.

Body, heart, and soul.

It will all be claimed by the sea. Kai doesn't fear the sea anymore because she's taken on its power.

And I'm fire—even with all its mighty power, I can be easily extinguished with one crash of her waves.

What do you fear now, Kai? How do I protect you? Because I no longer care if I survive, only that you do.

It's not because I love her; I'm too fucked up for love. But because I believe Kai is truly better than me. She has the power to change everything in our world. She has the power to stop the cycle of Rinaldis and Millers battling each other for a dark world that shouldn't even exist.

And because the only way to keep my empire and who I am is to give her up now, not wait until the end of the game. The fucking would have to stop. The kissing. The touching. The connecting. All of it needs to end in order to keep myself whole.

But I can't.

I want her too much.

I'm about to lose everything to this woman.

And the sacrifice will be worth it.

15

KAI

Enzo Black is broken.

How did I not realize it before?

Yes, I thought he was a little fucked up like all of us are. His father did a number on him. I understand the feeling now that I know my father did the same or worse.

But how did I not realize he's as broken, if not more so than I am? He doesn't even think he is capable of love.

Of being loved.

Of loving others.

Of falling in love.

I know Enzo can never love me. We are enemies. We've both betrayed each other and will continue to betray each other in different ways, but he needs to heal enough to love again. He helped me heal so I could love him. The only way I will be able to truly walk away from him is if I know he can love another—even if that person isn't me.

I lie in Enzo's arms on the couch in his bar area. My head pounds from the amount of alcohol we drank last night, but not once did I truly feel drunk. I always feel sober around Enzo. *I feel alive.*

He snores gently beneath me, naked and adorable. *Why don't you think you are capable of being loved? Why, why, why won't you let me love you?*

I run my hand through his hair, outgrown and in need of a trim. But I like it a little too long, a little too messy. It fits him better. Enzo isn't perfect. He's far from it. When he fucks up, he does it in a huge fashion. But that's what attracts me to him. He may fuck up, but he makes up for it just as effortlessly. Life with Enzo is never boring.

I reluctantly climb off him, knowing I need a gallon of coffee to have a chance of ridding myself of this headache.

Enzo grabs my hand before I fully leave him. "Where are you going?"

"To get coffee to try to stop this pounding in my head."

He frowns and pulls me to him, touching my head as if he can feel the pain there.

"I'm sorry, baby. I knew we shouldn't have drunk that disgusting liquor."

I raise an eyebrow. "You seemed to drink it just fine after you got a couple of tastes of it."

He sits up, grabbing his own pounding head. "Ugh, I haven't had a hangover since I was fifteen and just getting used to the stuff."

"You really shouldn't drink that much. It's not good for you."

He smirks. "You aren't good for me. Should I stop you too?"

Oh, God, please no.

"No," I kiss him hungrily on the lips. "I think we both just need a taste of our poison."

He kisses me back, his tongue sweeping into my mouth and tasting every last drop of the alcohol in my mouth.

A buzzing sound stops both of us.

We look over at Enzo's cell phone lying on the floor next to us.

I moan.

The buzzing continues, and we know he needs to answer it. My cell phone still lies in the bedroom I have yet to use. I like having it there in case I need it, but I also prefer sleeping in Enzo's arms.

Enzo pulls me to his stomach as he reaches down and grabs the cell phone from the floor.

"This better be important," Enzo snaps into the phone.

I watch as he listens carefully and then ends the call without speaking.

"Who was that?"

"The real world calling. I need to start going to work on a plan to take out Milo and every man who would step into his place. His empire is similar to ours. Ending Milo won't end the war. There is always another heir ready to take his place. I have to destroy the entire clan."

I nod. I know he needs to work. It's the only way we will ever get off of this yacht. Although, after last night, I don't plan on ever leaving this yacht again.

He hesitates as he opens his mouth.

"What?" I ask.

"I really don't want to include you in the Milo stuff, but I will if it's what you want. I know you are strong and very capable with a gun. But this fight is going to be between men that have been firing guns their entire lives. Used to hand to hand combat. Know how to wield a gun and a hundred different ways to kill. These men watch others die on a regular basis, and I don't want you anywhere near it when the time comes.

"I promise to share the important details of the plan once we have one, but I don't want you spending any more of your time thinking about Milo than you have to." He strokes my cheek. He thinks Milo is who I dread more than the sea. He doesn't realize the only thing I fear is losing him and having my heart ripped out because I fell in love with the wrong man.

"Go, involve me in what you want to include me in."

"This isn't a tactic to get another penalty against me in the games, is it?"

I laugh and kiss him quickly on the lips. "Maybe." I waggle my eyebrows.

"I'll win, even if I have to take a penalty."

"Who is ahead again?"

"You are, baby." He kisses me again and then throws my clothes at me. "Get dressed if you want to leave this room."

I sigh but put the clothes on. Someday we are going to have a place where I can go naked everywhere.

I shake my head. *There I go again, planning for a future that will never exist.*

Enzo dresses too, and we head toward the door that leads to the rest of the yacht and the world. We open the door, and as always, it seems like the entire yacht's passengers have decided to greet us.

Enzo frowns when he sees Liesel, but I need to stop putting off the inevitable. I need to talk to her. She's Enzo's friend. He obviously cares about her, and I need to know how much. I need the two of us to at least get along, and maybe she can help me understand Enzo better if I befriend her.

"Hello, Liesel, would you like to join me for coffee while the boys work?"

She grins. "I'd love to."

Enzo, Zeke, and Langston all frown at my idea.

"I don't think that's the best idea. Why don't you join us, stingray?" Zeke asks, always protecting me.

I smile at him and wish Liesel would find Zeke or Langston attractive and within her reach, instead of looking at Enzo like he's already hers.

"No, Liesel and I need some female bonding time. We are tired of the boys running the show all the time. You guys go play with your fancy computers and guns and leave us before a while," I say.

Zeke tells Enzo with his eyes that he hates it and he can stay back to keep an eye on us.

Langston shrugs, as if to say he's not getting in the middle of it. *Smart man.*

And Enzo turns to me, seeing there is nothing he can say to make me change my mind.

"Behave," he says, kissing Liesel on the forehead like she's his.

Chills of jealousy course through my veins. It was just a friendly kiss on the forehead, probably to try and persuade Liesel to be nice to me more than anything else.

Enzo looks to me, and I know he wants to kiss me on the lips to show Liesel just how much he's taken by me, but he thinks better of it. Instead, he kisses me identically to Liesel. On the forehead, but he doesn't tell me to behave. In fact, his eyes tell me to give her hell.

I smile. I know he wants the two of us to get along, but I can't, not until I understand what Liesel means to him.

The men reluctantly disappear, leaving Liesel and me alone.

"Change into your swimsuit and meet me upstairs in five minutes. I'll make sure Westcott has plenty of coffee to help you deal with the bags under your eyes. You want to hear my story. You'll get everything you want. And you are in desperate need of a tan. Your skin is far too pale," Liesel says.

I freeze, looking at Liesel truly for the first time. She's already wearing a gold and black bikini with a see-through white sarong around her hips. She has a full face of makeup, and her hair is curled in thick blonde ringlets. Her hair was darker the last time I saw her, but now she's dyed it a lighter shade of blonde. And to top off her look, she's wearing heels. *Fucking heels! Why?* We are on a yacht in the middle of nowhere, not going to the Met Gala.

But reluctantly, I agree. I haven't swum in the pool or laid out at all since we got in the yacht. If I'm going to understand this woman, then I need to do it on her terms.

And the only way I can truly understand Enzo is to know more about his past. Enzo will never face the fact that he needs to heal as much as I do, but maybe Liesel will be able to tell me how to repair him before it's too late.

16

LIESEL

I sit down on the lounger looking up at the sun. There isn't a cloud in the sky. This should be my heaven. Sunning myself on one of the most expensive yachts in the world. Instead, it's my hell.

Because the only man I've ever loved is here with another woman. A woman he could love if he ever let himself love again.

I hate her. She's competition. And she could destroy Enzo.

But I also love her for loving him. I can't fault her for falling for him. *I did.* Enzo isn't easy to love. He fucks up as much as he does right. But when he lets you into his inner circle, nothing can feel better than being protected by him.

Kai obviously loves Enzo. It's easy to see. I understand the feeling. I've been in love with him since we were fifteen. And the one month I got to date him was the best month of my life.

My heart broke when I realized I loved him and he could never love me back—that's Kai's fate. Loving a man incapable of love.

I'm not much of a saint. In fact, I'm the opposite of a saint. I have a law degree, and instead of helping the innocent, I work for big banks ensuring they, and I, get richer. I like money. Enzo has given me plenty to live off of, but when the love of your life has been taken from you, you find other things to pretend you love to occupy your time. And I love the thrill of chasing money, pretending that fancy cars, high-end clothes, and big condos are what get me up in the morning. That somehow those things will love me back.

"What can I get for you, Miss Dunn?" Westcott asks as he stands over me.

I shade my eyes to see him. "Coffee for Miss Miller and a pitcher of mimosas."

He nods. I'm surprised he hasn't already brought me a mimosa. It's what I've had every morning here so far as I sit by the pool by myself, with Zeke or Langston stopping by every once in a while to give me an evil look like I'm the bad guy.

They may have decided Kai has the best chance at getting to Enzo's heart, but they forget, I used to be her. I used to be the best and worst thing for Enzo. And all it did was rip out my heart and make Enzo put up more walls, ensuring no one ever gets through.

"Is this seat taken?" Kai asks.

I shield my eyes again as I look up at the scrawny woman standing in front of me. She's wearing a simple black bikini that looks like it came from Target, it's definitely not designer. She doesn't have any shoes on, and she's wearing a baseball hat to shade her eyes.

She has jet black hair. I have blonde.

She's a bit of tomboy; I'm a princess.

Her body is covered in scars; my body shines from all the plastic surgery I've gotten to hide mine.

We are so different, yet exactly the same. Both broken and hopelessly in love with a man who is more broken than either us. Because his emotions run deeper than either of us have ever felt.

I force a smile on my lips and nod to the lounger next to me.

Kai sits just as Westcott returns with our drinks.

"Iced coffee, for you, Miss Miller," Westcott says, handing her a glass. "And mimosas to share." He places the pitcher on the end table between us and then pours each of us a glass.

"If you need anything else, I'll just be in the kitchen, and I'll check on you soon," Westcott says.

I nod and sip my drink, waiting for him to leave before I speak.

"You look like shit," I say, not sugarcoating anything. That's not my style; I'm blunt and honest to a fault.

"Oh, um, I thought this was going to be a civil conversation where we try to get along for Enzo's sake. I'm sorry if I was mistaken, I'll just go," Kai says.

"Sit down," I say, jerking on her arm to keep her in the chair as she tries to get up. "I'm not trying to be a jerk; I'm just honest and have no filter."

Kai glares but doesn't say anything.

"I'm not going to apologize for anything I say either, so don't expect that. All I was trying to say is that you've been through hell, and it shows."

Kai narrows her eyes. "That doesn't sound any better than what you said before."

I sigh and lift my hair from my neck where a scar similar to the one she will wear forever on her neck lies.

Kai's eyes grow big, and her hand automatically goes up to trace the thin line.

"I used to look similar to you—not as bad. I only suffered for a few months before my own savior came for me, but I have the scars. With time, I've hidden them. Most with plastic surgery. Some with tattoos." I hold out my wrist where the word *beautifully* is written in script over a scar on my wrist where I tried to kill myself rather than keep dealing with the pain.

"All I'm trying to tell you is that you and I are more alike than you may think. And I'm trying to prevent you the same heartache I once suffered."

"You look pretty happy to me," Kai says as her eyes travel over my healed body.

"You of all people should know you can't judge a book by its cover. I look happy, but I will never be happy again."

Kai bites her lip as she finally understands what I'm saying. "Tell me. Tell me everything. Enzo saved you. He took care of you. You loved him, and then he ripped out your heart."

I nod. *And the same thing will happen to you.*

"Tell me, I need to hear the truth. I need to hear it so I can let him go."

I shake my head. "You will never be able to let Enzo Black go. Trust me, I've tried. But hopefully, you haven't fallen as deeply in love with him as I did."

"Tell me," she whispers again.

I close my eyes, letting myself travel back to the worst moments of my life.

———

"THIS IS OUR NEW HOME, LADYBUG," Mom says, squeezing me hard to her chest as I stare up at the big dark mansion.

It's ugly and big and horrible. It looks more like a medieval castle than a home, and not the good kind. The kind with evil ghosts, and monsters, and dank rooms.

"What do you think?" Mom asks.

I can't tell her any of that. Mom has a job as a maid here. It won't pay much, but we get a free room in the guesthouse, and the money will be enough to feed us so I can't complain. And hopefully, the guest house won't give me the same creepy vibe the house does.

"I think we will have fun here."

She grins and squeezes my scrawny ten-year-old body tighter. "We will."

She lifts one of the two boxes from our car and carries it to the guest house. I follow, carrying the other box that contains all of our belongings.

This will be a better life. It has to be. *At least here we won't starve.*

We take the next hour to settle in before Mom announces she needs to get to work. She tells me I'm allowed to explore the main house, and the owners, a Mr. And Mrs. Black, have a son around my age I should go introduce myself to.

No, thank you.

I'll stay here and lock myself in my new room and decorate it. I've never had my own room before, and although I don't have any paint or decorations to style the room with, I have paper and crayons that will have to be enough for now.

Mom leaves, and I get to work coloring pages various pinks to line my walls. I can't paint them pink, but at least the pages will allow me to pretend the walls are pink.

I've colored twenty pages when I hear the noise. It's a sound I know all too well when we were living on the streets of Miami.

Gunshots.

No!

I saw the walls surrounding this property. I saw the men

who guarded it. I saw the security cameras watching us as we pulled up. This house was supposed to be safe.

We were supposed to be safe here.

I don't think; I run out of the room and out of the small guest house.

I know better. My best bet at surviving is to hide under the bed or closet until Mom returns. But she is all I have. I have to make sure she is okay.

I hear more gunfire, and instead of running away from it like I should, I turn toward it.

I find the door and enter the creepy house. It's too big, too dark, and too old.

More shots.

I run up the stairs.

"Mom!" I shout, hoping she will pop out at any second and then we can run away from here. I'd rather starve every night than deal with the threat of guns in our own home.

I don't see her anywhere. "Mom!"

And then I hear a different voice, that of a boy's and he too is crying for his mom. His cry is different. It's louder and more panicked than my cry. He doesn't long for her to be found; he longs for her to be taken. Because he too feels the pain that looms in the darkness of this house.

I creep quietly toward the door, needing to comfort this boy more than I need to find my own mother. I've never heard or felt such pain. And it draws me in even though I know how dangerous and stupid it is.

When I reach the door, the sight I see terrifies me. The door is mostly closed, only open a crack, but it's enough for me to wish I'd stayed in my bedroom and never left.

I see a man with demons in his eyes, standing over a boy who can't be much older than I am. The only difference is where I have scrawny arms; he already has muscles. But those muscles *are marked with bruises and scars. Scars I have no doubt the man standing over him caused.*

But that's not all I see.

I see a woman lying on the floor gasping for air as blood oozes from her body.

"Are you really going to make your mother suffer?" the evil man says.

The boy's hand trembles, and I see the shiny black metal gripped in his hand.

No! His father can't be serious? He wants the boy to shoot his mother. He can't.

But I look to the woman who is already so broken and bleeding so profusely. Even if the boy doesn't shoot her, she's going to die. He might as well put her out of her misery. The pain in her eyes is unbearable.

"You failed her. You were supposed to protect her. To save her. And you couldn't. You weren't strong enough to protect those you love," the vile man says.

I need to do something. Either go inside and try to stop it or run and get help. This is wrong. But I do neither. I'm frozen watching the catastrophe in front of me.

A shot fires. And I squeeze my eyes shut, not wanting to see what happened.

Slowly, I open them and see the boy now lying on the ground, blood oozing from his leg. He doesn't scream or cry like I would from being shot. He welcomes the pain, like the pain is helping him avoid the torment his mother is feeling as she dies on the ground next to him.

"Now, be a man and put your mother out of her misery. She's in pain, much worse pain than you are. Show her mercy."

The boy's eyes are filled with tears as he looks at his mother.

She looks back and tells him she loves him. Then she looks at the man and tells him she loves him too.

How messed up is that? *She still loves this man who is most likely responsible for her death and for her son's pain. But I realize then that you don't get to choose who or how you love. You can't prevent it or stop it, no matter how much a person fails you, you still love them.*

That's when I vowed I would never fall in love—never.

Finally, the boy lifts the gun with too many tears in his eyes, and he fires.

———

I FINISH the story and look at Kai, who is crying buckets. I would be too if I hadn't already cried too many tears for that broken boy. That boy who was hurt more than any person ever should.

"Enzo killed his mother?"

"No, his father did. Enzo simply pulled the trigger. But that was the day Enzo learned he could never love. He'd be punished for loving, alongside the person he loved. And that he wasn't strong enough to save those he loved. But it didn't stop him from trying."

———

I've STAYED AWAY from the boy since that night. He scares me, but his father scares me more. I hide in the guest room, doing my school work there so I never have to leave. I'm not even sure they know I exist. I don't let them see me. The house has too many ghosts and demons, and I've learned to stay as far away as possible. I won't even swim in the pool out back, even when I know the boy and his father have gone.

I've become my own ghost. I lock myself in my room and

pretend I'm Rapunzel locked away in a tower until her prince comes. But unlike Rapunzel, I will never be rescued.

Mother went into town to buy us groceries. And the water calls to me. The longing to swim in the beautiful pool pulls me out of the safety of my bedroom.

I think they were gone. They often are. The father takes his son out on missions for weeks at a time. I don't know where they go, just that they are gone. The sun seems to shine a little brighter over the house when they are gone.

Mom bought me a swimsuit only last week. A simple bikini for my newly starting to bloom body. I am a teenager now. And I deserve to get to leave my room. My mother has tried everything to get me out of the room, not realizing the danger lurking so close to our home. She doesn't realize the evil man she works for, or if she does, she pretends he would never turn his evil gaze our way.

So I take a chance. I put on the bikini, and I creep out to the empty pool. The pool is rarely used. The boy occasionally sneaks out to swim, but he never throws any parties. And the father never swims.

The blue of the pool practically sparkles, inviting me in. And so I jump in, not bothering to hide my splash. Mom said we were allowed to use the amenities. And I have occasionally seen staff use the pool when the father was gone so I know it is allowed.

But it still feels wrong to enjoy something so grand.

But once I start swimming back and forth, I realize how right it feels. The water feels fantastic, and my muscles ache to get some exercise.

I swim hard, imagining I am a dolphin swimming free in the ocean. I would gladly turn into a dolphin and trade my sad life to become an animal. It has to be better than my pathetic life where I am destined to become a maid like my mother.

I hear another splash, and I stop, hoping it's one of the staff members. When I surface though, panic shoots through me.

It's the boy.

Although, I'm not sure I can call him that anymore. He looks like a man now, even though he's not older than fifteen. His muscles are large and defined. He has a six pack, or is it an eight pack? I can't tell as half his abs are submerged under the water.

"I'm sorry," I say, swimming toward the ladder to climb out.

"Don't go, Liesel."

He knows my name. He knows I exist.

I stop and stare at him. "How long have you known who I am?"

"Since the first day when you saw my mother die."

"How?"

He shrugs. "It's my job to know about everyone who lives and works in this house. And my room looks down into your room. I watch you sleep most nights."

"Don't you sleep?" I ask, feeling like he's a vampire from Twilight or something.

"No, never."

I frown. No one can never sleep. You need sleep to survive.

"I like what you did to the room. The pink suits you, and I like all the glitter you added."

I blush.

And then our world changes. His father yells in the distance, and the boy's ears immediately perk, sensing the danger.

"I have to go, you should go inside," he says.

I nod. I need to avoid the man at all costs.

We both climb out of the pool. I didn't even remember to bring a towel, so I drip the entire way back to the guest house my mom and I are staying in.

The boy starts running toward the house. The boy that knows everything about me, but I don't know anything about him.

"Wait...what's your name?" I ask.

He hesitates, looking at me like I'm a lost cat.

"Black. My name is Enzo Black."

And then the boy is gone.

Black. It's such a dark name. A name meant to send chills to anyone who thinks of crossing him.

I smile, watching the boy disappear. Maybe living here will be more tolerable than I thought. The boy didn't say it, but I know he's been watching over me, protecting me from the darkness. He will keep me safe here. He will become a friend, and then my life won't be so miserable anymore.

The smile remains as I walk back to the guest house. I am so lost in my own little piece of happiness, I don't notice the shadow covering the door. I don't notice the man creating the shadow. I don't notice the evil finally come for me.

"Black!" I scream as the man's hands grab me. But I know it's too late. The boy won't be able to save me. Not this time. This time evil won.

17

KAI

I try to hold in my tears, listening to Liesel's story, but she makes it impossible not to embrace everything she felt.

Enzo's life was a nightmare. His father trained him to become evil like him. He forced him to shoot his own mother to end her suffering, and then his father hurt the only friend Enzo had: Liesel.

I know Liesel didn't tell me the story so I would feel sorry for her. She told me to better understand her and Enzo's relationship. She told me their history to teach me a lesson.

"Enzo's father raped or beat me several times over the next few months. It was the worst time of my life," Liesel says.

I swallow down my tears, doing everything I can to listen and understand her pain.

"Enzo's father did unthinkable things to Enzo. Tortured him in the worst possible ways to try and make him strong enough to become Black. But Enzo would rather have the pain himself than watch someone he loves getting hurt."

"He loved you," I say, agreeing.

She shakes her head. "He wouldn't let himself after what happened to his mother. The only people he ever let himself love are Langston and Zeke, and he only allows himself that love because they chose this life. And he knows whether he loves them or not, they are going to put themselves at risk right next to him."

I shake my head. "He loves you, Liesel."

"No, I tried for years to get him to love me like I loved him. When we were teenagers, he learned to piss his father off enough so he would torture him instead of me. He took the punishment meant for me. And of course, I fell in love with him for protecting me. But he wouldn't let himself fall for me.

"When we got older, I persuaded him to date. It didn't last long. And even though we were both screwed up, I fell hard. He was the one for me. He protected me. He saved me. He worshipped me. And he vowed to never let another man hurt me again. The fucking was incredible, and his lifestyle was intoxicating. But he never let himself love me. Eventually, he realized he was hurting me more than helping me by dating me, so he broke it off."

For the first time since Liesel started talking, I see tears in her eyes.

"I loved him, and he broke me. And I can't ever heal from that."

I want to tell her how sorry I am. I want to tell her how I understand. But I can't. It won't make her feel any better.

"Enzo can't save those that he loves, so he doesn't allow himself to fall in the first place."

"But he protected you," I say.

"Only after months of abuse."

I suck in a breath, realizing what Liesel is saying.

"Enzo can't protect those he loves.

"He couldn't save his mother.

"He couldn't protect me.

"He'd rather face the pain himself."

"What do you want me to do, Liesel? I know that's the point of the story. Some lesson."

She cocks her head, shielding her eyes from the sun so she can look at me. "Not a lesson, but a warning. Enzo will never love you. I know you've already fallen for him. But you have to let him go."

"And what if I can't?" I whisper, clutching my coffee in my hands like it's a lifeline.

"Then protect him like he would protect any of us."

"How?"

"You already know the answer to that."

I nod. I do. Enzo can't handle those he cares about in pain. He can't handle not being able to save them. He can't handle not being enough.

"Promise me you will protect him, put his needs above your own desire to play superhero," Liesel says.

"I promise," I say, knowing exactly what I'm promising. That I have to keep myself safe at all costs, even if Enzo gets physically hurt. Because that hurts him less than seeing me suffer.

Liesel and I don't speak again. We just drink and soak up the sun, waiting for Enzo to finish his surveillance of Milo's residence.

I thought this whole time I was the broken one. That I was the one who needed healing. Enzo may refuse to love, but he couldn't stop the feeling from happening. His love saved me. And maybe my love can heal him back.

But what happens if I were to succeed? If I healed him and showed him he is capable of loving? And that love is what makes life worth living. That he can't fear it. *Then what?*

Would he choose me, a broken girl who he has to fight for an empire? Or would he pick his childhood friend, who has never betrayed him?

18

ENZO

I KNOW everything there is to know about Milo Wallace.

I know he's as evil and cruel as my father was.

I know he already bought a new whore to replace Kai.

I know his mansion in Italy is impossible to tackle without risking suicide.

I know he owns several of my yachts and prefers the sea, like I do.

I know he's a monster I will soon kill.

And I know I need to go interrupt whatever is happening between Kai and Liesel, because both of them are strong-willed and not afraid of a fight. And if I leave them alone for too long, one of them is going to end up going overboard.

I walk to the pool deck and find them both tanning themselves in their bikinis while sipping on mimosas.

They aren't speaking, which might be a good thing. It means they aren't planning anything against me.

"It looks like you two have spent your time productive-ly," I say as I lie down on one of the loungers next to Kai. I'm wearing jeans and a black T-shirt, and there is no way I will last out here in the beating sun dressed like this. But I don't plan on staying long.

"We had a very productive time," Liesel says.

I put my hands behind my head, trying to seem relaxed, but I'm anything but. Not when two of the people I care most about have spent the morning together most likely threatening each other. "So does that mean you are friends now?"

"No, just not enemies," Kai answers.

I look at her, searching her eyes for more truth, but she's not going to give it to me. I look over at Liesel, and she's as much as a closed book as Kai is.

These women are my everything. They are both smart, beautiful, and fearless. They have both faced more evil than any person should.

I should have fallen for one of them by now, but I can't. *I can't love.*

And both of these women deserve more than I can give them.

I look at Liesel, my childhood friend I've tried to protect with my life countless times. Sometimes I was able to save her, sometimes I wasn't. But when we became adults, I vowed no one would hurt her. No one has. I've at least kept that promise.

And then I look at Kai, a woman I've let down so many times. And in many ways, I have failed more than Liesel.

Liesel learned a long time ago I'm not worth loving.

But I'm not sure Kai has learned the same lesson yet. I need to remind her we are enemies at the end of the day. That we are two people drawn together by the need to fuck, nothing more.

I want to go remind Kai of that lesson right now. Take her to my bedroom and fuck her hard instead of gentle, remind her I'm rotten to my core. But I don't want to hurt Liesel.

Liesel may know there is no chance at us having anything more, but I don't want her to think there is any chance I'll be with Kai either. I just want to fuck her.

"Go," Liesel says, dropping her sunglasses over her eyes, looking bored.

"Go where? We are in the middle of the fucking ocean, Liesel."

She raises her sunglasses so I can see her roll her eyes. "Go fuck her."

Kai freezes at Liesel's words.

Liesel starts shooing us away, and I'm not going to miss out on a chance to fuck Kai. If Liesel is okay with it, then I'm not going to miss this opportunity.

I grab Kai's hand and pull her to me.

She blinks rapidly, and I can already feel her pulse speeding just being in my arms.

"We should stay. It's not fair to leave Liesel all alone," Kai says.

Liesel laughs. "I've been alone my entire life. I think I can handle a few hours alone on this big fancy expensive yacht. Although, if we do ever decide to make port, I will be bringing some boy toys on for me to play with. It's only fair."

"Come on," I tug on Kai's hand. Liesel is a big girl. She knows I want Kai. And whatever these two talked about while I was gone didn't change anything. They still hate each other and with good cause. I used to fuck Liesel. She used to be everything to me. And that makes Kai jealous. But now I'm with Kai, and that pisses Liesel off.

I can't win. I'm an asshole. I deserve any grief I get from either of these women.

I hold onto Kai's hand as I pull her down to our cabins. She doesn't resist, but she doesn't walk willingly either.

I unlock the main door to our cabins and slam her body into the door as it shuts, caging her in with my body and raging emotions.

I didn't realize how badly I wanted her until Liesel pointed it out. Something about hunting an evil man who wants to take Kai from me turns me into a caveman who wants to show the world Kai is mine by fucking her over and over again.

Kai crosses her arms though, seemingly pissed at me. That isn't going to save her.

"That wasn't very nice."

"I would think by now you would realize I'm not a very nice man. In fact, I'm very bad. And I want to be bad with you right now."

I move in to kiss her neck.

She slaps me.

Which only turns me on more.

"What did Liesel tell you?"

"Everything."

I nod.

Liesel knows my past better than anyone. She could tell all my secrets. And it appears she did. And now Kai is going to look at me with pity. I don't want her sympathy. I want her fire.

"It doesn't change anything," I say.

"It changes everything."

I narrow my gaze, and then grab her wrists, forcing them up over her head so I can kiss her without her stopping me.

I don't want to talk about feelings and emotions. I don't

want to talk about how I'm as broken as she is. I just want to fuck until we both forget about everything.

My tongue dances over her bottom lip, teasing her and letting her know I have all the power, and there is nothing she can do to stop this. I know all her buttons to press. I know what turns her on, and that pressing those buttons will send us into an endless spiral neither can control. Once we start, her mind will be shut out, and she won't want to stop us.

But her eyes turn into dangerous blue orbs as she bites at my tongue before I can retreat.

I growl as she holds her grip on my tongue.

When she releases, my tongue darts back into my own mouth. Afraid of the vixen taunting me with her perfect body in her skimpy bikini.

"Really? You don't want me to fuck you?"

"You have to beg first," she says, batting her long eyelashes.

Not going to happen, baby, I don't beg.

"Fine, you aren't the only woman on this boat. I'm sure Liesel will have no problem playing. She was, after all, looking for a boy toy to play with. And she knows how good I am in the sack," I say, releasing her and going for the door handle.

Kai slides in front of the door with a scowl I've never seen on her face. Not even when I betrayed her by selling her to Milo.

"You are the biggest ass on the planet."

"And you are the most stubborn. You want to fuck me, so why are you denying yourself?"

"Because we need to do more than just fuck. I have things I want to talk to you about."

"I'm not in the mood for a game of truth or lies, sweetheart," I say.

She hisses. "I don't want to play a game. I want to talk."

I shake my head. "Not going to happen. Now, do you want to fuck, or should I go find Liesel?" I wouldn't really fuck Liesel. I would just find a bottle of bourbon and drink with her until the sun fades. But Kai needs to know she isn't my boss. *I am.* Liesel may have shared my past, but that doesn't mean I'm willing to talk.

I stare at Kai who is just as stubborn as I am, and I know I'm not getting laid.

I reach again for the handle, but Kai shoves me back. I barely move, her body is about a tenth of the size my body is, but I step back giving her room.

"Fine, have it your way, asshole," she says.

She stalks toward me, and I back up like I'm fucking prey. The look of intensity on her face tells me to not stand in her way.

"You think that's all we are to each other—fuck buddies?" she asks.

"Well, we are also enemies fighting each other for a game."

She narrows her gaze and stops as my body collides with a wall.

"We are so much more," she hisses.

"I'm your protector. I'm your enemy. I'm your fucker. Nothing more."

"You're also my fucking drug. I want nothing more than to storm out and show you that you can't just demand I fuck you whenever you want. But one hit, and I'm yours. I can't quit. I want hit after hit."

My eyes darken with heat. "And you're my addiction. One I need to give up for my own survival."

She reaches her hand behind her body and undoes the ties of her bikini top. I watch as it falls to the floor, giving me the perfect view of her gorgeous tits.

"Then what are we going to do?" she asks.

"Fuck each other until one of us overdoses."

Her eyelids grow heavy as I remove my shirt and she takes in my sculpted abs. Her gaze drifts to the v that dips into my pants. And her breath hitches.

I love that I make her body respond like that. She can't control how her body reacts to me.

"I'm the only man who makes you feel this way," I say, caging her in again.

"Yes."

I hover close but don't fucking touch her. When I touch her, an explosion will go off.

I know it.

She knows it.

And I'm prolonging the feeling as long as I possibly can.

"I'm the only man who can touch you and give you pleasure and not pain." My lips almost make contact with hers, but I stop them.

"Yes." She pushes her bikini bottoms down, completely vulnerable to me.

I undo my jeans and push them down, retrieve a condom, and put it on. My cock is already hard, and I haven't even touched her yet.

I look between her legs and see the moisture. She's dripping, already demanding for me, and I haven't even kissed her.

My cock will be the first thing that touches her.

I stare at the condom I hate. I want to feel her skin to skin. But I don't dare get her pregnant.

She spoke once about not being sure if she could

conceive. But in order to fuck her without a condom, I would need to have a serious conversation with her. Possibly call a doctor to look at her, and I don't want to share anything more serious with her. I've already led her on too much.

I will protect her, nothing more.

And fucking her without a condom would be more.

"Turn around," I command.

She does, sticking her ass out, pushing it so close it almost brushes against me.

She turns her head in my direction, her big eyes anticipating the collision of our bodies in a fierce battle neither of us will be able to quit.

I lick my lip instead of hers like I want—the anticipation taunting both of us.

For a woman who doesn't like being touched, her body is begging for me to grope her all the fucking time. We are magnets pulling toward each other, but also ripping each other away from everything else in our lives.

I stare at her ass.

"Don't you dare," she says.

I chuckle. "Your ass will be mine someday soon, little virgin. I will take all of your firsts.

"I took your first kiss.

"I took your first touch.

"I took your first fuck.

"I will take your ass."

She stiffens.

"But not today. Today, my cock is begging for your dripping pussy."

Her shoulders relax, and that's when I take my cue.

I plunge inside her and ignite the spark that only exists between the two of us as I find her tight walls with my cock.

"Jesus, fucking Christ," Kai cries, not from me pushing her pussy too hard, but from the fucking sweet electricity pulsing between us.

Everything ignites.

The pleasure.

The shock.

And emotions that shouldn't exist.

I don't know what this feeling is when I'm in her; the only thing I can describe it as is home. I feel at home when I'm in her. But not the kind of home that comforts and protects you, the kind that pushes your boundaries and creates a chaos of emotions.

I grab her hips, needing more connection as I push into her deeper.

Her legs spread for me, and her ass pushes higher as her face pushes into the wall.

"God, why do we ever stop fucking?"

"I don't know. We should never stop," she purrs.

I move my lips over hers. Tasting her purity and desire pouring from her lips. I get drunk on her lips as I thrust into her.

And the cries leaving her throat tell me she's lost in me.

I slap her ass, watching the pinkness spread and intensify our connection. My heat pushes through her cold, and I can practically see the spark of energy from the firm touch.

"God, it's too much."

"Never."

I slap her ass again as I thrust.

Her body trembles, and I know she's trying to hold onto her orgasm so this feeling can last longer. But it's impossible to hold onto. Just like us, the feeling is fleeting. Every day is a gift, and tomorrow it could all be taken away from us.

"I can't hold on," she cries.

"Then let go."

She bites down on her lip, trying to wait, but it's impossible to hold onto. She lets go. Her orgasm ripples from her head to her toes. Her body trembles. Her body flames. Her pussy tightens, coming hard on my cock.

And as much as I want to hold on, I let go too. Spilling everything I have into the condom still deep within her core.

I need a bed to collapse into, I'm so spent from fucking her against the wall. She is too. I wrap my arms around her, holding her up, knowing I'll need to carry her to a bed.

She has her own bed she might want to sleep in. I gave her the choice of freedom, but tonight I'm not giving her that choice. And she's never once chosen her bed over mine anyway.

So I lift her body and cradle her as I carry her to my bed. As soon as I regain my strength, I will fuck her again, and that's easier to do if she's here in my bed instead of hers. I would have to break her door down to get to her otherwise.

I climb into bed next to her as the buzzer on my door goes off. I really need to have that removed.

I dig my phone out of my jeans I threw on the floor next to the bed to see who is at the door.

Archard.

Fuck.

"What's wrong?" Kai asks, so in tune with my emotions right now I couldn't hide anything from her.

"It's Archard."

She frowns.

I press a button on a panel that connects me to the outside.

"What do you want, Archard?" I ask.

"I need to speak to both you and Miss Miller."

I'm not about to let him into my personal cabins or anywhere near a naked Kai again.

"You are speaking to both of us," Kai says, reading my thoughts.

I see Archard's reluctant face. He wants to talk to us in person—too fucking bad.

"Tomorrow. The next game will happen tomorrow. You won't have to leave the ship. But you will face your greatest weaknesses. Those you care about and love will be at risk. And you won't be able to save them, even from yourselves," Archard says.

Kai and I exchange glances at the warning for the game. The clue proves a problem because Kai no longer has anyone she loves. Her father was the only person she loved, and after his betrayal, she hates him.

And I am not capable of true love. Sure I love Zeke and Langston. I care about Liesel and Kai, but my father, who created this game, wouldn't know about my feelings for any of them. And the clue specifically said love; my father made sure I never loved anyone.

Love equalled weakness to my father. And my father made sure I never showed weakness by doing something as stupid as falling in love.

19

KAI

ARCHARD'S WORDS haunt me all night.

Someone I love is going to be hurt, and there is nothing I can do to prevent it.

It scares the crap out of me.

And I don't sleep one second all night.

Enzo doesn't either.

But neither of us talk about what the game could be. He just holds me in his arms all night.

After our first fuck, we both intended to spend the rest of the night fucking each other's brains out. But after Archard spoke, we couldn't. They only way we could have had sex would have been slowly, intimately, and vulnerably. And neither of us wanted that moments before we were going to have to compete.

So we didn't.

We didn't speak.

We didn't fuck.

We simply held each other all night, both of us dreaming about what tomorrow was going to hold.

Hurt someone I love.

The only person I love is Enzo.

But I doubt I will be the one hurting him.

And Enzo loves no one.

I thought he did, and he just didn't show me. But after hearing Liesel speak, after fucking him so hard last night, I know he truly doesn't love me. He can't love. His heart is too broken to love. Whatever his father did fucked him up in a way I'm not sure I can fix him. And that breaks my heart.

We've been living in the shadow of Milo hunting us. So consumed by running from him and trying to figure out how best to kill him that we both forgot about the game. And that we were going to have to compete against each other.

I'm the first to leave the bed.

I'm the first to shower and get ready.

The first to declare us nothing but enemies.

This round is going to be harder than the first. The first round, my father chose the game. This round, Enzo's father designed it. And somehow, despite my father being the man who sold me, I think Enzo's father may have been worse.

The game Enzo's father chose for us is going to be much harder than the first. And even after one of us wins, who knows what the consequences of that win be.

After the first game, Enzo sold me because he thought I betrayed him. It led to a war we will eventually have to wage against Milo.

That was before I realized I had fallen for him. Now that my heart is involved, I don't know how I'm going to handle any pain Enzo exerts against me during the game.

It's just a game. We don't have a choice. I can't let anything Enzo does get to me.

That's what I continually tell myself as I walk to the main deck where Archard is waiting for us—alone.

I walk over to Archard without a word, dressed in dark jeans and a gray T-shirt. My hair is pulled back in a low ponytail. I might as well have painted war paint on my face, because that is what I'm preparing for—war.

Enzo approaches Archard as well. Dressed similarly, jeans, boots, and a dark T-shirt. The only difference is the bulge in his waistband where he carries his gun as always.

Unlike last time, Langston and Zeke aren't by his side. He comes alone. Most likely because he is no longer sure if Langston or Zeke would be on his side or mine. Or maybe he's trying to make the fight fair this time.

Enzo's eyes hold the weight of the world—like he is walking to his own funeral. He knows his father better than anyone. And he knows that whatever his father planned for us is going to kill, or at least ruin, us.

Archard looks to each of us, then down at a piece of paper in his hands. The paper has the rules of this game on it. The paper will destroy whatever relationship Enzo and I have built.

"Get on with it," Enzo growls, no longer having any patience for this game or process.

This is only the second game. And already it's too much for either of us.

Archard doesn't react, completely unfazed by Enzo's outburst.

My eyes snap to Enzo's, and I see the worry and pain in the frown lines of his face, and my stomach flips again, knowing whatever we will face will be personal in a way the last game wasn't.

"If you will follow me, Mr. Rinaldi," Archard says to Enzo.

Enzo frowns as Archard begins to walk away.

"What about me? What about the rules?" I ask, not liking being left out.

"I will share the rules when I get back. The game is to be told to each of you individually," Archard says.

I hate it. If we are told together, then maybe I will get some clue from Enzo about how to handle the game. But now, we will both be in the dark.

Enzo doesn't look back as he follows Archard into the depths of the yacht. I'm left standing on the main deck alone, with nothing but the warm salty breeze to keep me company.

Why couldn't the game be something easy, like chess? Some sort of strategy game that determines how well our brains work. But I know that isn't what this is. Whatever awaits me in the rooms below deck is dark, and most likely, the cruelest thing I have faced yet.

Alone I stand.

Alone I wait.

Alone I tremble.

The wait stretches, and the fear creeps into every nerve in my body. I'm shaking, I'm cold, and I'm worried.

But I can't let the fear win. This is part of Enzo's father's plan. I will not let him destroy me, not like this.

I close my eyes, already feeling my body shut down. Maybe, just maybe, I can use that to my advantage for once. I don't want to shut everything down; I won't be able to do any task that way. I need to feel, just not the fear.

Let it go.

Let it out.

I feel the fear as I push it out of my core. And I focus on Enzo.

The love I hold in the depths of my heart is everything. I didn't let myself feel that love before—not fully. But I do now. Because his love is the only thing that might save me.

I force myself to feel instead of shutting the world out. Feel the torture I felt when I watched Enzo walk away from me and not knowing what he was about to face. Feel the love I felt when he held me in his arms all night, the man who shot and killed a man for wanting me. Enzo Black may be most people's hell, but he's my heaven.

Archard returns silently, my eyes are still closed, but I can feel him near me. Because he brings Enzo's pain. I feel it as clearly as I feel my own heartbeat.

Enzo is in pain. The kind that will stay with him for the rest of his life.

Fuck.

"Is there any way to stop this? Can I just withdraw?" I ask, my eyes still closed.

"You can withdraw, but Enzo would still have to complete the rest of the games himself in order to keep the empire. Once the games have started, there is no stopping it," Archard says.

Fuck Enzo's father. Fuck my own father. Fuck generations of our families before us, wanting us to play this twisted, vicious game all so the strongest would rule the empire. *Fuck it all.*

"Are you ready, Miss Miller?" Archard asks.

I laugh. Such a ridiculous question. I'm not ready —never.

I open my eyes until I'm sure the blue in my irises has turned to red. That's all the answer Archard is going to get. But it seems to be enough.

He starts walking.

I follow, the fear gone, replaced by rage. Enzo is hurting, and there is nothing I can do except end this game as quickly as fucking possible. But if I win, then that puts me up two to nothing. I don't want the empire. I can't handle ruling. Enzo deserves it all.

It's a no-win situation.

I push those thoughts out of my head for now. I don't even know what the game is yet; I need to focus on that first.

Archard goes to one of the cabins I've never been in before. I know this is where most of the crew sleeps, in cabins near here.

He opens the door silently and holds it open for me to step inside.

Zeke.

He's standing inside looking as clueless as to why he's standing there as I am entering the room.

He's wearing the usual uniform of jeans, boots, and a dark T-shirt. His hands are in his pockets, making the muscles in his arms bulge. The man is huge. Like Jason Momoa huge. And Zeke has the long locks to match tied up in a man bun.

Is Zeke here to help me complete this game?

That should comfort me. Instead, the butterflies in my stomach return in the form of wasps, stinging, and raging in my belly.

"This game is simple and is all about testing the belief that you are able to put the Black empire first, above everything that you hold dear," Archard starts.

Zeke looks at me with a nervous expression. We both know where this is going.

"If you were to become Black, you need the ability to extract important information out of any man you capture. No matter if they are your enemy or friend."

Please, no.

"Zeke has a past, a secret he has never told anyone, even you, Miss Miller."

No, no, no.

"Your job is to extract this secret via any means possible," Archard continues.

FUCK!

"You can use any tools or weapons you deem necessary to extract this information." Archard points to a table in the corner with various weapons.

Shit.

I can't use any of that on Zeke. And even if I wanted to, he's stronger, more powerful than I am.

"You can bring in any person you need to help subdue him, but you are the one who has to do all the torturing. And you can torture him, even to death, so as long as you get the information."

I can't bring myself to look at Zeke as I feel the tears in my eyes. There is no way I will be able to hurt him.

"Who does Enzo have to torture?" I ask, my voice stronger than I feel.

"I'm sorry, but I'm not allowed to tell you that information. That is part of the game. Enzo doesn't know who you are torturing, and you don't know who he is torturing."

But I already know who he's torturing, the only person he would give his life for—Liesel. *His everything.* I saw how her contact was written on his phone when he was scrolling absentmindedly through his phone last night, trying to distract himself from what is to come. It broke my heart at the time, now it destroys me.

"Any other questions?"

"So the winner is whoever extracts the information first?"

"Yes."

I can't let Enzo hurt Liesel.

But I can't hurt Zeke.

There has to be another way.

"I have monitors in both rooms I will be watching. I know the information each prisoner contains, and I'll know when that information is extracted. Otherwise, there are no rules."

"I don't get to know what information I'm looking for?"

"No."

Archard walks to the door, "When the fog horn sounds, you may begin."

And then he's gone, locking the door behind him.

And I'm left alone with Zeke. But I still can't bring myself to look at him. I need a second to breathe, to think, to find a way out of this mess before I lose my soul by torturing a man who doesn't deserve it.

The fog horn sounds, giving me no time. Not enough time to figure out how to save us all.

And then I hear a scream so loud it sends vibrations through the entire boat. A cry that will live inside me forever. A cry of a heart breaking.

Enzo's cry, scream, growl all rolled into one. It's a cry of a warrior about to face a battle. The cry of a man so destroyed by what he has to do. And I know I have limited time to save Enzo. Because there is no way he's going to back down from this challenge, even if it destroys him in the process.

———

THE FIRST THING I do is walk to the door, testing to see if I'm locked in.

I am.

I'm trapped in this nightmare.

And the only way to get out is to torture one of the few people in the world who loves me.

Slowly, I turn to face Zeke, who is still standing there with his hands in his pockets. He's still weak from getting attacked before because of me. And scars etch into his tan skin. I can't cause more.

I bite my lip as I try to figure a way out of this. It's just a puzzle I need to solve, that's all. I don't have to torture anyone.

"What is your secret, Zeke?" I ask, maybe it will be that simple. Zeke cares about me, loves me even, not in a romantic way, but in an—I'm your big protective brother who will beat the shit out of anyone who touches you, sort of way.

"I can't," he says.

I frown. "Why not? You care about me. You definitely care about Enzo. He's in the other room right now, torturing Liesel. She's suffering. He's suffering. You can end it all if you just tell me."

"I can't," he repeats.

"Why not?" Maybe the secret is truly so big he can't spill it. Even to save himself. To save me. To save Liesel. To save Enzo.

We don't speak, just peer into each other's souls. *What are you hiding, Zeke? What is so important you can't tell me to stop the pain?*

"Because you can't win," he finally says.

"What?"

"I can't let you win."

I frown. "But I thought..."

Zeke walks over to me and puts his arms on my shoulders, like I'm the one who needs comforting instead of him. He's the one about to be tortured.

"I can't let you win because I love you, Kai. And I love Enzo too."

I nod. "I know that."

"And I can't let you win, because you deserve better than this life. Enzo doesn't know anything different. He doesn't know how to handle his problems without using his fists or a gun. You haven't killed anyone. You are still innocent and pure. You can be free when these stupid games are over. You can find a life with true happiness. And if I tell you my secret, then you will be one step closer to being trapped in this life forever. I would never forgive myself if I did that. Enzo would never forgive me. And if you are being honest with yourself, you would never forgive me."

"Will Liesel give away her secret to help Enzo win?" I ask, my voice filled with hope.

"No."

"Why not? She'd rather him win than me."

"Probably, but I know what her secret is. She'd rather die than share it with Enzo."

"Enzo won't torture her. He loves her," I say.

He doesn't blink as he says his next words, "Not as much as he loves you."

My eyes water. I've wanted Enzo to show me he loves me this whole time. I want him to tell me he loves me. But not like this. Not by keeping me from torturing a man. Not by keeping me innocent. Not by hurting the only woman he ever loved before me. Not by breaking his own promise to her to keep her safe.

"Don't hurt her," I send out a plea to Enzo. If neither of us tortures our prisoner, then neither of us can win. But then I'm pretty sure we'd all die in these cabins, because I'm sure the rules that Archard is following states to not let us out of these rooms until one of us has extracted the secret.

"What do I do?" I ask Zeke.

He opens his mouth to speak but is interrupted by another horrendous scream. Liesel's scream.

Fuck, I'm out of time to decide. Enzo has chosen. And he chose to torture Liesel.

I feel the tears drop down my cheek as a tiny crack in my heart forms. Enzo isn't perfect. Far from it. But I love him. I love how fiercely he protected me, even from himself, *but can I forgive him for hurting a woman as broken as I am?*

Zeke's eyes are filled with moisture too, and I know his heart is breaking just as mine is, but he won't relent. He won't tell me his secret, because he needs Enzo to win, at all costs. And the cost this time, might be too great.

"What do I do?" I repeat my question.

"Whatever you need to," Zeke answers.

Whatever I need to.

What I need to be able to live with myself.

What I need to do to save Enzo.

Because he is the man I love above all else.

I love him. And I won't let him torture Liesel, and in turn, destroy himself.

I love Enzo—I would eventually forgive him for this. That's what love is.

But Enzo doesn't love anyone, including himself. He won't be able to forgive himself for this. And I know that pain is something he will never be able to stop living with.

I walk over to the table and examine every weapon. I run my hands over each of them, feeling the pain they will enact with only a touch because I've felt every one of these weapons myself. I've felt the pain.

I close my eyes, sucking the tears back inside as I pick

up my weapon. Already knowing my soul is about to turn black. My heart and soul are about to be given to the devil, freely. I'm about to curse my soul to hell, all to save a man I love. And I'm going to deserve every moment of fire and torture I'll get.

20

ENZO

MY SCREAM IS primal and evil and love and sacrifice and fucking everything. The scream sucks my life from me, while also energizing me.

And I curse my father who is burning in hell for creating this disgusting, cruel game.

But then what did I expect?

My father prepared me my entire life for this exact game. Which is why I learned to never truly love another person, so if I was forced to hurt them, it wouldn't truly matter because I wouldn't love them. My heart is guarded from the world because I don't love. And the world is safe from me because I can do what is necessary to prevent truly evil things from hurting the innocent, even at the cost of my friends.

But there is just one problem with my plan. Somehow along the way, my heart opened, maybe not enough to love, but enough to make vows of loyalty. Vows that tiptoe on the edges of loving another person.

I've only ever made two vows in my life. One to protect Liesel. The other to save Kai. And I'm about to break one of those vows today, because I can only save and protect one of them.

This shouldn't hurt me; my soul is already stained black. I already surrendered my heart to the devil years ago, when my mother died because of my gun. Because I couldn't save her.

And if I don't decide quickly, I won't be able to save either woman.

"What is your secret?" I ask Liesel. Hoping she will spare us all a lot of pain by just fucking telling me. But then Liesel was never one to save me back. I've protected her countless times, but she's never protected me. Not that I deserve anyone's protection.

"I can't tell you," she says, crossing her legs as she takes a seat on the chair I'm meant to interrogate and torture her in.

"Why?" I growl.

"Because I want to protect you."

I scoff. "You've never wanted to protect me before."

Our eyes burn into each other, sharing our pain, the love we could have had if we weren't both raised in this fucked up world.

"Fine, I want to protect myself. I want to protect what little love you have for me, because if I tell you my secret, it will break you. You will hate me, and I can't live with your hate," she says.

Finally, the truth.

Hearing Liesel's truth is so different from when Kai spills a secret to me. When Kai tells me a truth, it's because she wants me to know her better. When Liesel tells a truth, it's to hide more of herself from me.

"Tell me, Liesel. Make this simple, easy. Get back at my father. You hate him as much as I do. It would be like killing him all over again if we defied his game, and I learned your secret without hurting you."

She smirks, looking bored. "It would be great revenge."

Yes, please, just tell me. I don't even care what it is. Just tell me.

"Tell me your secret. Whatever it is won't change things between us."

"It will break your heart."

"You forget, I don't have a heart to break."

"That's a lie, and we both know it."

I frown. *Come on, Liesel. Just tell me.*

I reach into my back pocket and pull out my phone and scroll until I find her number. Then I hand it to her. Hoping to pull on her heartstrings.

She stares at the phone, at the name I've given her number in my phone.

My everything.

Liesel tears up at the contact entry. She never cries. Never. But she does now.

I kneel down in front of her. Knowing this could be it— the moment where I win a game before it even starts.

"You see, there is nothing you could tell me that I wouldn't forgive you for. You wouldn't even have to ask for my forgiveness; I would just give it—freely. I give it now, before you even tell me, because there is nothing you could say that would make me feel differently about you. You are my everything. You have been since your big brown eyes showed up on my doorstep when we were ten. You mean the world to me. I've vowed to protect you, to never let anyone hurt you, including me. Don't make me break my promise to you."

Liesel reaches out and touches my heart, feeling the unrelenting pounding in my chest. I wish I could say it was beating so wildly because of her. Maybe then she'd tell me her secret, but it's beating for Kai. Longing to go rescue her from her own torture in the other room.

Because I know who's she's trapped with—*Zeke*. A man she's formed a bond with I can't understand. It could be Langston, she's formed a relationship with him as well, but Langston is still mine, while Zeke has become hers.

I send out a silent plea to Kai. *Don't you dare touch him. Just wait. Let me win this one. I'm so close.*

I don't send the plea because I'm worried about Zeke. He's withstood plenty of torture before, and I know Kai can't physically hurt him too badly. But because I don't want Kai to relinquish the part of herself that is pure and innocent. The part of herself that makes her her. The part that is holy and sacred and hers. If she sacrifices her soul, it will only be for one reason. To save me. And I don't deserve her saving.

I look down at where Liesel still rests her hand against my chest. I take her hand calmly and bring her palm to my lips. I kiss her palm sensually.

"Please," I beg. "Please tell me. I already forgive you for whatever it is."

"You're a liar, Enzo Black."

I frown. "I'm not."

She shakes her head, hands me back my phone, and then pulls her palm from my grasp.

"I'm not your everything, not anymore. And you will never forgive me."

"Liesel, please," I beg again. I've never begged a woman so much in my life. But there is only one woman I would beg like this for: Kai, the woman who means sea itself. A woman that has conquered the sea, along with her fears and my heart.

"Please," I whisper one last time.

"I can't."

I stand, closing my eyes and turning away from Liesel. And then I let the darkness in. It doesn't take much, it's always in my heart, locked in the deepest part. It takes everything I have to keep the evil in and not let it out without me telling it to be free. But it's always there. Always ready when I need it, even when I don't.

It's the part of me that escaped its cage when I thought Kai had betrayed me. And I almost burned us all down in the process.

It's why even when I have to do evil things, I rarely let the monster out. I prefer to handle all the cruel things myself. I let myself feel every drop of pain, but that only feeds the monster more.

But this time, the only way I'm going to be able to hurt Liesel and save Kai is by letting the monster out.

So I do.

I stare at the table filled with weapons, and the monster laughs. I don't need a weapon to torture Liesel. Even the cruelest part of me isn't that cruel to hurt a woman in that way. And even if I did, Liesel is too strong to be broken with knives, whips, or guns.

She's faced it all at my father's hand and never broke.

But I know what Liesel is truly afraid of because I know her better than any other man. And I know I won't have to lay a finger on her to force the truth from her. Because the threat of pain is worse than the actual pain for her. And I know how to play with her head to get to the truth.

"Stand up," I say not turning to look at her, keeping my voice calm and cool.

The monster is out and ready; my body is flaming with the fire always burning inside me. What I wouldn't give to touch Kai right now and steal some of her cold, cool calmness.

I pick up the rope, the only weapon I will touch.

And then I turn to face Liesel, sliding the two strands of rope into my back pocket so she can't see which weapon I chose.

She's standing almost eye to eye with me in her ten-inch heels. I used to admire her for looking so fierce in shoes and outfits like the one she's wearing. A dark red dress and shiny silver shoes that make her look like sex and nothing else. But now, I see nothing but the scared little girl I saw in the hallway all those years ago when she watched me shoot my mother to end her pain—the moment I let the monster in.

Liesel stands not because she chooses to follow my orders, but so I can see the defiance in her eyes, and I know how much I'm going to have to break her to end this. And have a chance at saving Kai from creating her own monster.

"Back up," I say, taking a step forward.

"No," she says defiantly.

And then I use a voice I've never used with Liesel before. A voice I hate.

"Back up," my voice booms, bringing with it the fire of hell.

She stumbles back, the fear creeping over her now pale skin.

My eyes blaze with the fury my father put inside me all those years ago. I stand taller as the monster grows inside me.

I take another step, pushing Liesel back with my body without touching her because she fears what I might do to her. She stops when her back hits the wall behind her.

"Strip," I growl, my voice low.

She grips her dress and pulls it over her head quickly. And I can see what she thinks, that seeing her naked will somehow turn me on and make me stop this. I won't hurt her when I remember she's a woman, and I don't hurt women.

But I don't lust after Liesel, not anymore. My cock only points toward one woman these days—Kai.

Liesel smirks, but it doesn't reach her eyes as she stands naked in front of me except for her shoes. Her long flowing hair and large tits make her look all woman, and sexy as a goddess. But it does nothing to my body. My cock doesn't even stir.

"Turn around," I say low and breathy.

She smiles and does as she spots the rope I bring out from my pocket.

"Kinky," she says.

"No, Liesel. I am anything but kinky right now."

I don't want to do this, but I must. I won't lay a finger on Liesel. Not one finger. I'll only make her think that I could. That I will. That I'll hurt her.

"Give me your hands."

She extends her hands behind her back, and I tie them, careful not to touch her skin as I force her wrists together. And then I bend down and tie her legs.

"You're my prisoner, Liesel, nothing more."

She scowls at me as I look at her.

And I know the way to break her. Not with threats of fucking her, but with threats of never touching her. Of her never being enough. Of her meaning nothing to me.

I take a step back as she turns around, balancing precariously on her heels, now that her feet are tied together.

"You're nothing but a sick bastard. You're just like your father," she spits out.

I grin. "I'm nothing like my father. My father wanted you. He raped you. He took your innocence. I want nothing from you."

Her face drops.

"I want nothing but your pain."

She narrows her eyes, trying to understand what I'm doing, but I see her fear. I see her pain. She's exposed to me, and I see all of her.

I take out my phone, pulling her number out again, I type in the change to her contact.

"You are nothing," I say, showing her my phone.

"Take it back," she sobs.

"No, you are nothing. Nothing but the daughter of a maid—*my maid.* You should be cleaning this yacht, not living the life of luxury in your penthouse condo."

"Stop."

"The only reason you have anything is because of me. Because I let you. I let you leave my house. I paid for your college. I got you into Harvard. Me—not you."

Her eyes darken, and I see the fierce fire. Let it out *Liesel, let it go, stop making me hurt you.*

"I ensured your grades were straight A's by bribing your teachers. Every friend you ever met was me. I paid people to befriend you."

"Liar."

"Am I?" I walk toward her, and she tries to hop away, but it only gives me room to circle her like she's prey.

"Then how come you know I speak the truth? Everything good in your life was because of me, and I didn't even care about you. I still don't. You were just a puppet for me to play with."

"Stop," she says again, this time her voice is weak, not fierce. *We are getting closer.*

"You were my father's greatest fascination, and my biggest pain in the neck. It was fun watching my father play with you though. And you enjoyed it, didn't you?" I seethe against her neck.

"I didn't," she cries out loudly, so loud I'm sure everyone heard her.

Fuck, I hate myself. I hate myself so much for this.

End this. Now.

"Admit it, you've hated me this entire time that I've hated you. Since the moment you met me and saw me kill my mother, you hated me. All of your supposed feelings for me were just a trap. Just a way to gain knowledge about me to use later. So you could hurt me later."

"No," she whispers, her voice weak as her head drops.

"How does it feel?" I purr over her shoulder.

"What?" she looks up.

"To know that you are nothing."

I hook my foot under the rope tying her legs together and pull. She collapses to the floor, dropping to her knees before me. If I was my father, I'd make her suck my cock. She is at the right height for it, after all. But I'm not my father. I never will be.

But then why do I feel like I am?

I walk behind her and squeeze my tears down because I feel every drop of Liesel's pain. And I hate it. I hate myself. I hate my father. I hate all of it.

End this.

Stop the pain.

"How does it feel to know I chose Kai over you?" I circle back to the front so she can see me. See the pain and thinking all of my pain is for Kai, and none of it is for her.

I stand tall over her, looking like the complete demon that I am.

"How does it feel to know I broke my promise to you because of her? I will always choose her over you."

And then I choose the words that will break her. The words will be a lie, spoken full of truth.

"How does it feel to know I love Kai when I could never love you?"

She sobs. All she has ever wanted was to be loved by me. And I could never give it. She thought it was because I could never give it to anyone. And she was right. I can't. But she thinks I love Kai in a way I could never love her.

"I hate you," she finally says from the floor, naked, exposed, and vulnerable.

"I know; as I hate you."

Then the fire returns, and I prepare myself for the storm she's about to blast me with.

"I could have saved your mother," she shouts.

Her truth.

Her secret.

It guts me, just as she said it would.

"How?" I growl.

She couldn't have, could she? I killed her with my bullet. She was dying, and I ended her suffering.

"Your father and you left your mother to die on her own, but I stayed. I watched. I snuck into the room, and she was still alive—very much alive."

No, that's not possible.

She sits up straighter, watching how her truth hurts me. "Your mother begged me to save her. To get help. I could see that although you shot her, it wasn't fatal. She would die a slow death, bleeding out. She collapsed to the floor when you shot her so you could think you were saving her from the pain by putting an end to her suffering. But she didn't die."

"Why didn't you save her? Why didn't you call for help? My father and I left the premises that day. You could have saved her. Called an ambulance. Nothing was stopping you."

And then I see the monster in her eyes. I wasn't the only one who gained a monster that day. "Because I saw the pain in her eyes. I saw the evil. She still loved your father despite everything he did to her. She loved him—the monster, the devil himself. And because she loved him, I couldn't let her live. So I left. I let her die on that floor alone."

I close my eyes holding in my pain. It's not fair to hate Liesel. We were young.

My father was the one who started it all.

He shot her.

I finished her.

Liesel left her.

We all betrayed my mother. We all played our own little part. And nothing we do now will bring her back. The only woman who could ever love me. She may have had her faults when it came to loving my father, but she loved me and that's all that matters.

I reach into my boots and pull out my knife.

Liesel's eyes go big, thinking I'm going to hurt her with it to get my revenge, but I will never seek vengeance when it comes to her.

I slice through the ropes, freeing her, and then I remove my shirt and pull it down over her arms, dressing her like a broken doll. Because she's as broken as Kai and me.

The pain of her words hurts me, but I deserve them. Because I hurt Liesel. And she will never forgive me for it, just like I can't forgive myself for hurting her to win a stupid game.

So I turn and walk to the door that unlocks now that I've succeeded in my mission.

I won the second game, but somehow, I also lost. I let the monster out, and now that he's free, it's going to take everything to cage him again.

I let the monster win, and I lost everything in the process.

Fuck you, father.

21

KAI

I PICK UP THE GUN.

I know it's the deadliest weapon. The only one I know how to yield because Zeke taught me.

How ironic that one of the men responsible for teaching me how to use a gun will be the first I use my skills on.

Ironic and sad. Because I don't want to hurt him. But the only way to save Enzo from himself is by ending this—fast.

As quickly as possible.

The other weapons would only draw it out. I don't know how to use a whip. I've thrown a knife, but that was mostly luck, and I can't get that close and hurt Zeke. He's not tied up. He would never let me hurt him. The only weapon where I can keep my distance and still hurt him is a gun.

I hold the metal in my hand, hoping that me holding it will be enough for Zeke to change his mind. Enough for him to stop this.

"Don't make me hurt you, Zeke. End this. I will have only won two rounds. I won't win more than two rounds. I don't want to be Black any more than you want me to."

"I can't. We don't know what the next round will be. We

189

don't know if Enzo will be able to beat you. I can't let you win this round," Zeke says, still keeping his hands in his pockets. He doesn't look afraid. Not one bit. He doesn't think I'll shoot him, but he forgets how much I love Enzo. I will do whatever I can to save him.

"Enzo is strong enough. He can win at anything."

Zeke shakes his head. "He's strong, but so are you. You are more equal in this fight than either of your fathers ever imagined you would be. Enzo may have grown up in this world. He may be better prepared, but your father prepared you more in the single day he sold you than Enzo's father prepared Enzo over the course of a lifetime. You developed more strength in a single day facing that kind of pain and loss of control than Enzo ever has."

I hate Zeke for speaking the truth.

He stares down at the gun I'm loosely gripping. "You'll shoot me; I don't doubt it. You might even kill me in order to save Enzo. You love him. You want to protect him. But you forget you aren't the only one who loves him. I love him too. And I love you. And I will do what I can to protect you both —including die. My life means nothing compared to yours."

Who hurt you, Zeke?

"The love between you two is epic. It's the kind of love that only happens once in a million times. A love that will bring about change. Maybe it will end the world, or maybe it will save it. But it's that big of a love. You have already figured that out, and as soon as Enzo stops fighting it, he will realize he loves you too. And once you declare your love to each other, you will be unstoppable."

Tears, dammit.

So many tears pour down my face. Zeke is as hurt and broken as Enzo and I am. *Why didn't I realize it before? Why did I let him get hurt the first time?* This would be so much easier if I didn't already care about Zeke. If I hadn't already betrayed and hurt him.

"Dammit, Zeke," I say, dabbing at my eyes with my shirt.

He smiles gently, like the gentle giant he is. Any woman would be lucky to love a man like Zeke. He shouldn't give up his chance to save Enzo and me.

I hold up my hand; the gun pointed at Zeke as I feel my time running out. Already, Enzo could have hurt Liesel. He could have whipped her. Beat her. Hurt her. And I can't let him.

"Please, Zeke, just tell me," I whisper through my tears.

"It's okay," he says, knowing what I have to do, but it doesn't change what he does.

"If you say you want to save the love Enzo and I have, then you won't make me do this, you will end this. You will stop Enzo from hurting me, because if he hurts Liesel, I will never forgive him."

Zeke cocks his head. "Yes, you will. You love him. Love can forgive anything."

My hand shakes. "I can't forgive this. I've already forgiven too much."

"It's okay, Kai. I'll forgive you. Enzo will forgive you. And you will eventually forgive yourself."

My heart breaks so far open I'm not sure I can put it back together. A giant hole forms, endangering everything I care about.

Not time.

Not love.

Nothing will fix it.

I'm permanently broken. Because I have to choose between two men I love, and I already know who I'm going to choose—Enzo.

And that breaks me more than anything. Most love isn't

tested like this. Most love isn't this big. Most love doesn't require you to give up everything and everyone you love in order to keep that love. But my love for Enzo does.

Our love is toxic. It's wrong. As Zeke said, our love is destined to destroy the world.

All the more reason to let go of it. *Save Zeke. Choose Zeke. Let Enzo go.*

But saving Zeke means I'll end up alone—never to fall in love again. Because Zeke is right, the love I feel for Enzo is a once in a million kind of love, and once I've felt that I will never settle for anything less.

But I'm selfish to keep Enzo's love even though it will end up destroying me and everyone else who enters our lives.

"Zeke," I warn, as I blink away the tears.

Zeke takes a deep breath as he ties his hair back, and then he closes his eyes, putting his hands in his pockets, letting me hurt him.

I swallow.

I can do this.

I can do this.

I can do this.

But when I fire, more of me breaks. I only graze the outside of his shoulder, but it's enough to cause pain and for me to know I've sacrificed everything because there is no coming back from shooting someone you love.

"Ready to talk?" I ask. *Please.*

"No, never, stingray. You're not strong enough. You can't hurt me," Zeke taunts—trying to make me shoot him again. Trying to take away some of my pain. But then he shouldn't have used his adorable nickname for me if he wanted me to shoot him.

Fucking, dammit.

It only makes me love him more.

I aim again, this time for his other shoulder.

And then the door opens.

I turn with wide eyes as I see Archard standing at the door.

"The game is over," he says.

I drop the gun so fast I'm afraid it will go off from the impact when I realize I didn't put the safety back on. But thank God, it doesn't.

It's over, all over.

The relief that washes through me is everything.

But then, I realize what it means. *Enzo hurt Liesel. He got her secret.*

And it crushes me.

First, I walk over to Zeke and examine the flesh wound I caused on his shoulder.

He laughs, shaking me off. "I'm fine. You barely hit me. If that's your aim, we need to practice some more. If you are torturing someone, the goal is to shoot them where it hurts."

His words are meant to make me laugh, to make me feel better, but they don't.

"Hey, stingray." He lifts my chin with his finger. "I forgive you, but honestly there is nothing to forgive. You were protecting Enzo, and I love you even more for that."

He pulls me into a hug before I can argue.

We are okay.

This won't come between our friendship.

Even though it should.

Even though it hurt me to hurt him.

Even though the cut is only skin deep, it's enough to know what I would have done.

"Go," he whispers, knowing I need to see Enzo. I need to find out the truth. I need to know what he did to win.

Archard has already left. So I run out searching.

Nothing.

There is nowhere to go down here except our rooms. And I don't think Enzo went there. At least not until he has officially been declared the winner.

So I go up. Up to the top deck and I find them—Archard and Enzo.

I walk slowly over. Enzo won't meet my gaze. In fact, I'm not sure he recognizes I am here at all. And I can't feel him like I usually can.

I can't feel his cold.

I can't feel his love.

I can't feel his pain.

"Good job, everyone. Round two is officially over," Archard says.

I hiss when Archard says 'good job' like we are competing in a track event.

Fuck him.

"Enzo is the winner. That means you are tied—one to one. I will schedule the next round soon, determined by Kai's father. Until then, I guess it's back to sailing the ocean,"Archard says trying to lighten the mood. But the mood will not be lightened.

Archard realizes he is no longer welcome and leaves us alone on the small top deck. The deck has the best views, but the smallest surface area. It is empty except for the two of us.

Enzo still doesn't look at me. He hides—like a coward.

"What did you do?" I ask.

Finally, he looks at me. And the anger etched there is not what I was expecting.

I was expecting pain, agony, regret, and the need for forgiveness. Instead, I got rage.

So I push more. "What the hell did you do?" I step into his space, filling it with my own anger.

"I won. What the hell does it look like I did?"

I see the sweat on his brow. The bulging of his veins. The grip of his hands. Whatever he did to Liesel was physical. It was painful and required all of him.

I take a step back. "I can't believe you hurt her."

He growls at my words. "Does it shock you, that I'm a monster? I thought you had already learned that lesson, baby."

"Don't call me baby," I say, and I feel the hole in my heart expanding. *Bigger, bigger, bigger.* If it gets much bigger, it will rip completely in half. As it is, I'm not sure I can forgive him, and I don't even know how he hurt Liesel, just that he did.

"What. Did. You. Do?" I ask again. I need answers. I need to see the monster. I need to know how big of a monster I am when I forgive him.

His eyes dig into my soul and pull out my truth. "The same as you. The only difference is I was faster. I found my monster sooner."

"I hate you."

"Good, at least we agree on something."

"Stop!" Liesel's voice booms over everything. We both turn in her direction as she stands at the top of the ladder that leads up here, looking more like a girl than the sexy woman I know her to be.

She looks at Enzo. "You don't get to hate yourself. You did what you had to do. What you did wasn't that bad. I'll heal, I always do. Just give me a few days."

Then she glares at me. "And you, you don't get to be

pissed. You don't get to determine if you forgive him or not. There is nothing you need to forgive. She lifts the T-shirt I realize is Enzo's to reveal her untouched body. I hadn't even realized Enzo wasn't wearing a shirt; I was so consumed with my own pain.

"He didn't hurt me, at least not physically. He found another way to get my secret. And my secret hurt him more than it hurt me." Liesel stares up at the man we both love. "And he chose *you*. He saved *you*. His father forced him to choose, even from his grave. He saved you. He kept his promise. Don't hate him for it."

And then, she's gone.

And I know her words are the truth. I shouldn't hate him because he did save me from completely ruining myself. From physically harming Zeke. He found a way to save us all with the least damage done.

"You hate me, truth or lie?" Enzo says.

I think for a second, but I already know my answer. "Truth."

He nods.

"You hate me, truth or lie?" I ask.

"Truth."

I swallow hard. We both hate each other, but only because of how much we love each other. You can only truly hate those you love, and I know now that Enzo saying he hates me might be the closest I ever come to hearing him say he loves me.

Taking away the hate isn't about forgiveness. We don't need to forgive each other. Our love just lives on a spectrum between love and hate. Right now, our feelings are at one end of that spectrum, and someday they will end up on the other end. It's when one of us stops loving each other and removes themselves from the spectrum that my world will end.

"Show me your hate. Show me your pain. Take it out on me. Use me," I say.

He shakes his head. "No, I'm going to my room. I'll see you when I see you."

I move in front of him, preventing him from going anywhere. "Did I ask you? No, I told you. Use me, and I'll use you right back."

I push hard against his bare chest, and my hands instantly burn. His skin has never felt as hot as it does right now. And I realize it's because the devil inside him is out right now, and he doesn't know how to cage it again. That's why he burns. And if he's not careful, he'll burn himself down, along with everyone on this ship.

"You're hot."

"You're wet," his eyes dip down to between my legs.

I roll my eyes. "I meant temperature hot."

"I meant soaked like you just got caught in a rainstorm."

I bite my lip. I was always taught never to play with fire, but I have a feeling playing today is going to do more than get me burned. Playing today will mean giving up everything to the fire and letting it consume me.

But maybe my ice is enough to save myself, at least this time.

"I'm warning you I will destroy you if you don't let me pass. I will take everything and never give it back. I will burn you to the ground. I will feed on your fears and show no mercy."

"Good, because I have no fears left to feed on. And I've always wanted to tame a beast."

I move in to kiss him hungrily, planning on nipping and

biting my way over his body. But he catches my chin in his hand. *Fuck.*

"I'm not here for your kisses," he says.

"Then what do you want?"

His eyes heat. "I want you to pay for what I had to do to Liesel."

I grab his jeans, jerking our bodies together. "Oh, I'll gladly pay, and take everything I deserve from you."

I grab his cock through his jeans. "Because your cock will be my payment."

He gives me an evil smile, and my body tingles, trying to figure out what is going to happen next.

His hands go to my T-shirt, ripping it expertly down the middle.

T-shirt.

That's when I remember Liesel was naked except for his shirt. *Naked!*

And now I'm pissed off.

I grab his balls and twist.

He jerks and winces at my grip.

"You fucking bastard. Did you fuck her? Is that how you got her to surrender her secret?" Although, I don't think fucking Liesel would have convinced her to talk. She wants to fuck Enzo.

"I didn't touch her."

I don't stop twisting.

"Lies."

He shakes his head and spins me around, pushing my stomach into the railing and my ass into his throbbing cock. "Oh, baby, when will you learn to tell the difference between when I'm telling the truth and lying?"

He grinds into my backside. "My cock only gets hard for you." He rubs it into me until I can feel just how hard.

"I made her strip so she would feel vulnerable."

He jerks my pants and panties down until I'm naked.

"I tied her up so she would feel at my mercy."

He pulls my hands behind my back as if I'm tied up.

"And then I pulled the truth from her with lies," he whispers into my ear.

I hear his pants going down.

"But I tell you when I'm lying, and when I'm telling the truth. And I don't plan on speaking much longer. I plan on fucking you until you fear me again. Until you want nothing to do with me. Until you run away, because now that I've let the monster free, he won't go away. Not without a fight. And you will get hurt in the meantime."

And then, we are falling. Down into the fucking ocean. To the place Enzo still thinks I fear. But I don't. I don't fear the ocean, especially not with Enzo wrapped around me.

The water is the same temperature as my skin, which means it must feel cold to Enzo. The surface of the water consumes me in one gulp. The impact of the water separates us for a second as we become submerged under the water.

I open my eyes, knowing the salt water will sting, but I don't care. I want to see him.

And when I do, it feels like magic. Like we are the only two people left in the world swimming in the depths of the ocean. Enzo's eyes meet mine, open just as wide despite the pain, and I see everything—the pain, the fear, the love.

He's as scared to love me as I am to love him.

But we don't live our lives letting fear win.

It's more than the dread controlling his love. At least it's not his fear, but his fear for me. All those he loves end up hurt by him or his enemies.

Liesel is the latest casualty. He didn't physically hurt her, but he still caused her pain her even after promising he never would.

I know. I know you can't love me.

And then we both break the surface, breathing in air we both desperately need.

We don't connect immediately, the connection we had under the water was enough to overwhelm both our senses.

And suddenly just as fast as we took the dive into the water, Enzo is upon me, running his hands over my naked wet body.

"You really aren't afraid?" he asks. His question has a double meaning. *Am I afraid of the water? Am I afraid of loving him?*

"No, I'm not afraid of the water," I say, because the other question I'm terrified of.

He nods, understanding.

My legs go around his waist as his cock presses between my legs begging to be let in.

I want nothing more than to let him in, but fucking in the ocean, as romantic as it sounds, is very difficult to actually do. I want to press my lips to his, but I realize from his expression he still won't let me. He doesn't want to let me all the way in. So I'm left clinging to him with my body, hoping it's enough for him to feel the emotions I reaching out for him.

"We have to swim," he says suddenly.

"What?"

He laughs, realizing I haven't noticed our predicament. He nods in the direction behind me. I turn and realize the yacht has continued moving away from us.

Shit.

But why, despite my brain fearing the yacht stranding us

in the middle of the ocean, does my heart not care? *Because I'm with Enzo.*

Enzo reads my mind.

"Swim, we will figure the rest out later," he says.

He waits, and I start doing the breaststroke, not sure if it will be enough to catch up to the yacht, but surely someone will notice us both missing soon and stop the yacht or turn it around to search for us.

I swim hard with Enzo by my side. And I swear the only thing missing from my perfect piece of heaven would be if some dolphins came up next to us and started swimming, leading us back.

Instead, it's just the two of us. And it's the first time in years I don't fear the ocean. Even if we died here in the water, this moment would be worth it. This moment of connection with a man I love. That's what I want out of life —love. I realize how empty my life was before without it.

And I'd rather have love and die young from heartbreak than spend a long, lonely life without love.

We both stop automatically as we near the yacht. As I suspected, someone noticed our absence and stopped the yacht. We climb up on the back, soaked, exhausted, and naked.

But it's not time for rest.

Enzo pushes me down onto my back as his body engulfs me. We don't have a condom, but neither of us cares. The chances that I am capable of getting pregnant are slim. What's more important is this connection.

Enzo enters me, and my entire body feels home again. This is what has been missing from my life, and I'm never letting it go.

Milo will have to pull Enzo from me with all the force of the world to keep me away from him. And I know that Milo doesn't have that kind of power. The kind is bigger than anything of this world. That's the kind of power needed to separate me from Enzo.

He thrusts so deep inside me I can't distinguish from where he ends and I start. I've never felt so connected to him.

"The games can't hurt us," I start as he thrusts silently.

"The truth can't hurt us," I continue.

"The lies can't hurt us," he finishes.

"Because we have something greater—"

Enzo doesn't let me finish my sentence. His lips crash down on mine. Taking my breath away with a kiss I've been desperate for. A kiss I needed more than I needed air. And the kiss is everything. It is love itself even if Enzo would never admit it out loud.

Nothing can hurt us, not anymore, because we have something greater...

22

MILO

"Sir, Rowan Evans is here," Vito says, stepping into the office.

I sit in my chair behind my desk—pissed and angry.

I don't know why the man who stole Kai from me wanted an audience. But I allow him to come, if for no other reason than I can shoot him in person.

The door opens again, and Rowan steps inside.

"Well, isn't this a surprise. I didn't think you would ever be willing to face me, not after what you did," I say.

"Did I hurt you?" Rowan asks, his eyes searing.

"Not physically, but you took from me."

"And it earned me Enzo Black's trust."

I study him. "Why do you hate Enzo Black?"

"Because his father took someone I loved from me—my wife. And I swore on her life I would get retribution. He's already dead, but I'll settle for killing his son."

My eyes darken. I was ready to kill this man for taking from me, but I might be willing to forgive the sin if he helps me take down Enzo Black.

"I assume you gave him the whore back?" I ask.

"Yes, but she's not just a whore. She is so much more."

I huff. "I don't care if she's a fucking princess. I want to steal her back and make her my whore. Then I want Enzo Black to die slowly, and watch him suffer."

He smirks like he thinks I'm a fool. *How dare he!*

"Kai is Katherine Miller, Kai Miller. We all thought Enzo had already fought to claim the title of Black. But we were wrong. She's the woman he has to fight for power of his empire."

How did I not make the connection myself? She really is a princess, and what she could inherit is more powerful than inheriting any throne. The Black empire makes more money than most small countries. It has men and spies in almost every country. But that is not where the Black empire shines. The technology that has been developed for security purposes is greater than anything else. That's why I buy all my security systems and yachts from him. But I know Enzo keeps the best technology for himself, that way he is always protected.

What I could do with that kind of power! If my empire were melded with his, I would be unstoppable.

"But the girl can't have a chance at winning, not against Enzo," I say sadly, realizing the girl really has no use beyond my initial plan.

"I heard you are missing a ring," the man says, staring at my empty pinky finger. "That was the first task. She won. She stole it."

An evil grin forms on my face.

"They are tied—one to one. The first to three wins. Enzo is strong, but so is Kai. And with your help, the girl could win."

I nod, a new plan forming. I can now see why Enzo was

so fascinated with her. She's his enemy. And she equals him in every way.

I need to steal her. *Or I need to steal him.*

I need to threaten something she cares about to ensure she is on my side. *Or threaten someone he cares about.*

I need to train her to win. *I need to force him to fight for me.*

I need to weaken Enzo. *I need to weaken Kai.*

I need to take the Black empire. It doesn't matter which of them I choose. I have leverage on both Enzo and Kai. And I won't need either for long, just long enough to win the empire.

That's the endgame—getting Black's empire. And Rowan will help me accomplish that.

"I have a plan, and you are going to help me enact it."

Black is about to lose everything he cares about. His friends, his family, his woman, and his empire. And only when he's lost everything will I rest. Only when Enzo Black is nothing but a name people whisper in memory will I stop.

23

ENZO

It's been weeks since I won the game.

I thought the game would destroy us, but instead it healed us. And something happened inside me in the ocean with Kai I can't explain.

It's like the ocean healed me along with Kai.

I've never felt so calm as I do now. I didn't think the monster would ever go back in its cage. And I don't think it did. Instead, I've learned to live with the monster free. And in turn, I've never felt so free myself.

I'm not the only one who has healed.

Kai leans over the railing on the top deck where we dove into the ocean together weeks ago. She smiles as she stares out at the blue abyss she has so much in common with.

Kai and I have healed—together.

I don't know what you would call our relationship. There is no label to accurately define our relationship. We aren't dating, we aren't boyfriend and girlfriend, we aren't married. We aren't in love. But our relationship is different than anything I've ever felt before.

I'm no longer in constant pain every day. I'm no longer guarding my heart or holding back any part of me. I'm free.

Our relationship isn't the only one that has healed.

Kai and Zeke have grown closer, until they seem closer than my relationship is with Zeke. They share secrets like they are best friends.

Langston on the other hand has grown closer to me as he sees his best friend grow a relationship with Kai, leaving him in the dust. Langston has grown more and more unsettled as the days pass, and I know he's missing the comfort of a woman in his bed. He used to enjoy countless dates and women in his bed every night. But here he can't have that. His playboy lifestyle can't exist here.

Zeke, on the other hand, is used to being alone. And having Kai welcome him so openly has brought him to life.

I don't know exactly what happened during the game. I don't know how Kai tried to hurt Zeke or why Zeke didn't just spill his secrets to Kai immediately to ensure she won. But Zeke doesn't look physically hurt. And whatever happened is nothing but a distant memory between them.

And even Liesel and I's relationship has mended. At least enough where we can tolerate being in the same room with each other. Liesel is no longer my everything, but she is still worth protecting. She's still a woman worthy of protection, even if she has secrets and pain like all the rest of us. That only makes her fit into my life more.

I walk over to Kai and lean against the railing next to her.

"Rowan wants to meet. I agreed. We need to end this fight with Milo," I say.

Kai nods. "I agree."

"You will stay here," I say, knowing it's a shitty move, but

I don't want to risk her. I trust Rowan, but I don't trust the sea. This yacht is the safest place she can be. Nothing tops the security built into it.

She takes a deep breath. "I knew that's how you'd feel."

"So you aren't going to argue with me about it?"

"No, as long as you make one promise to me. You won't hide anything from me. You will tell me your plan when it comes to attacking Milo. And you will let me participate in the planning. You will let me judge if the fight is too risky. I won't go with unless it's safe for me, but I won't let men fight on my behalf if it's too risky," she says.

"My life means nothing compared to yours."

Her eyes burn. "My life means nothing without you."

Love has never been spoken between us. The word doesn't exist in either of our vocabularies, but sometimes when she says things like this, I wonder if she feels it—love. But then just as easily, I dismiss the thought. We don't love each other. We can't love each other. This is still going to end with one winner and one loser.

"I need to go. I'm taking Langston and Zeke with me. They both need to know the plan and earn Rowan's trust."

"I'll be safe," she says.

"I know you will. Westcott has as many skills with a gun as I do. No one knows where the yacht is or that you are on it. And if you feel unsafe, go to your room. Take Liesel and everyone else with you. No one can hurt you there. The walls are impenetrable."

She kisses me softly on the lips. "Go, make a plan. The sooner you talk to Rowan the sooner we can all head home. Everyone is getting far too antsy as it is. If we don't go home soon, there might be a mutiny."

I smile and then disappear before I change my mind

and decide to spend my day fucking her again, like I have every day since the game.

I find Langston on the deck watching Zeke pull the small tinder boat around for us to meet Rowan away from this yacht. I trust Rowan, but I don't want him to know where Kai is. If one of his team members aren't as trust worthy as he is, they could tell Milo. And then we'd be fucked.

"Let's roll," I say to Langston as Zeke inches forward with the boat.

But Langston stops me. "I don't trust him."

"Rowan? I don't trust anyone fully, but he is our best chance at taking down Milo. He is the reason we have Kai right now."

"No, I meant Zeke."

"Zeke?" *What the fuck?* "He's like a brother to us. He's sacrificed his life for us."

"I know. But he's hiding something. When he did a surveillance run last week, he was gone longer than he should have been. He said he was checking out another yacht nearby, but our radar showed no other boats. There is something he's not telling us," Langston says staring at Zeke who has pulled the boat to us.

"Are you fuckers coming or not?" Zeke hollers.

I frown at Langston. "He is your brother. Trust him. We will be lost if we start fighting between ourselves. The three of us are family. Don't forget that."

I hop onto the boat and Langston follows.

I don't need Langston doubting right now.

I don't need Zeke losing focus.

I need everyone ready to take down Milo.

I need to protect Kai, and then I need to set her free as promised.

I thought I should wait until the end of the gan
the longer we are together, the more damage I'm going
to her.

She needs to be free. And the only way to set her fr
to destroy Milo.

24

KAI

I FEEL uneasy with Enzo gone.

Like a piece of me was taken. I feel unsteady and unable to live. It's like living under a dark cloud. Everything is in shades of grey and white. Color no longer exists in my world.

A storm has started to roll in in the distance, and I wrap my arms around my bare shoulders as I stand on the top deck looking out at the horizon where I watched Enzo leave with Langston and Zeke. They've only been gone an hour, but it feels like a lifetime.

"Here," Liesel says from behind me. She's holding out a shawl to me.

I take it and put it over my shoulders as I'm only wearing a bikini top, and short shorts cover my ass.

Liesel is dressed more conservatively in sweatpants and a long-sleeved T-shirt. I've never seen her dressed so down before. She's usually glamorous and sex on heels.

"You okay?" I ask. We haven't talked since the games. Enzo and her seem to come to some sort of agreement between them, but I know it's not the same as it was before.

Liesel doesn't answer me. "You know he's coming for you."

I frown. "Enzo? He's coming back."

She shakes her head. "Milo."

"How do you know that?"

"The same as you, we can feel it. People like us who have been hurt before. Who have experienced true danger. We can feel it in our soul when danger is approaching. It doesn't always help us escape it, but we can feel it coming."

"It's just the storm you feel."

She closes her eyes as the wind picks up.

And then I see it. The light of a large vessel in the distance headed our way. And I feel it in my bones. I feel what I've felt this whole time, but pushed out because there was nothing I could do anyway.

"Get everyone and head to Enzo's cabin," I say.

"We can't enter, not without you," she says.

Shit.

"I'll go unlock the door. Get everyone. Now!"

I run downstairs as I text Enzo on my phone. The first text message I've made since getting the phone.

ME: Milo is coming.

I RACE to the thick cabin door that is as secure as any bunker built for a president.

I unlock the door ,and then I wait. Westcott is the first to arrive. "Get everyone inside. Stay here and hold the door for everyone. I'm going to make sure everyone gets inside."

"You need to get inside. Let me and Liesel handle

getting everyone," Westcott argues. And I know Enzo has given him an order to lock me inside.

But if Milo comes I know he is coming for me. And I won't let anyone else die because of me.

I wiggle free of Westcott's hold easily and start running, Westcott tries to follow.

"Hold the door open, or none of us will survive," I order.

Westcott stops, staying by the door.

And then I run up pushing as many people as I pass down into the cabins as I can.

A buzz alerts me to my phone. I stare at it as Enzo's name pops up on my screen. I changed it from Giant Dick...

MY LOVE: Fifteen minutes.

I TAKE a deep breath feeling like a pirate about to have her ship invaded. I need to hold Milo off for fifteen minutes. I need to keep everyone safe for fifteen minutes.

It could take that long for Milo's vessel to get here.

But when I get back to the main deck, I know my time is up.

Milo Wallace is standing on the end of the pool deck with a cheshire grin on his face.

But no other men accompany him. He knows Enzo is on his way here. He knows if I wanted to, I could hide away in the cabins below, and I would be safe from him. But that wouldn't keep Enzo safe.

"I think you and I should talk," Milo says.

"I agree." And then I step forward, surrendering myself to someone worse than the devil, in hopes of saving my love.

25

ENZO

Milo is coming.

The text message both startled me and pissed me off.

We have a traitor. Someone on my ship, or Rowan's, betrayed us to Milo. It's the only way Milo would have known to attack while we were most vulnerable.

Fuck.

"We attack tomorrow," I say, ending the argument about when is the best day to attack.

"Agreed," Rowan says with a growl.

If Milo took Kai, I need to get her back as soon as possible. "And if he already has her, we attack tonight."

Rowan nods solemnly as I jump off his yacht and back onto my small boat.

We take off racing back to my yacht, and I hope to God Kai listened to me and went to our cabins. If she's there, she's safe.

I text Westcott, who I tasked with making sure Kai went to the cabins where it is safe.

. . .

ME: Is she there?

I WAIT.

One second.

Two.

My heart beats a million times in between each second.

WESTCOTT: I failed, sir.

FUCK.

"Faster," I yell to Langston.

And then I take my anger out on Zeke, the only remaining man. I pull out my gun and shove it in his face. I need answers—now.

Zeke puts his hands up, his body movements are slow and cautious, filled with uncertainty as he watches me wield a gun.

"Did you betray us? Did you betray Kai?" I ask.

Zeke frowns looking from me to Langston.

"I would never hurt Kai. I would protect her with my life. I would protect her even from you," Zeke says.

"Then what the fuck happened? How did Milo know to attack?"

"Rowan," Zeke says.

Fuck. And I know he's right. Rowan betrayed me to Milo.

"Why? Why would he?"

"Your father made many enemies, Enzo," Langston adds. "When we return, I'll do more research to see why Rowan would hate the Black name."

"Fuck!" I put the gun back in my pocket. Happy that

Zeke didn't betray us, but pissed that Rowan did and that I was stupid enough to trust him. Because it would be so much easier to take down Milo with his help. Now I have to face two enemies. Two enemies that are playing me.

And I will make them both pay.

We reach the yacht faster than fifteen minutes. I jump onto the yacht with my gun drawn, ready to face Milo here and now, but I find the yacht empty.

No other yacht is near. *He's gone.*

If he took Kai, I'm going to do more than just kill him. I'll kill everyone he's ever met.

And then I see her, standing out at the front of the boat, like a goddess protecting all on her ship.

"You're here," I breathe out relief and run to her to throw my arms around her body.

"Yes, Milo left as soon as he saw your boat approaching. He was just trying to scare us and let us know that he knows you have me," she says.

My hands run over her body, looking for any evidence of injury, I run my hands through her hair, touching her scalp, her face, her neck, her arms. Then over her stomach, hips, and legs.

"I'm okay. He didn't touch me. He was just threatening us, letting us know our time is up," she says.

"His time is up."

"You have a plan?" she asks.

"I have a plan. But it doesn't involve Rowan. I think he's a traitor. I think he's on Milo's side."

"Then how are we going to defeat Milo without Rowan's help?"

"I have a plan," I lie.

"Tell me."

I promised to tell her, but I can't. I don't want to worry

her. I don't want to make promises to her I can't keep. And the only promise I've made so far is that I won't let another man hurt her. And I won't. *I fucking won't.*

Instead of answering her with words, I answer her with my lips.

I kiss her so hungrily I don't know how her lips don't detach from her body.

She throws her arms around my neck, clearly okay with me distracting us with sex instead of answering her questions.

But I don't want to fuck her here. I want to fuck her in her bed where she belongs. And where she will stay until Milo is dead. And I've dealt with Rowan.

I grab her ass, and she throws her legs around me easily without a fight. She wants me as badly as I want her.

Our lips dance with each other, vicious and reckless as I carry her from the upper decks down to ours. We pass plenty of my crew on board, but they quickly move out of the way.

When I unlock the door to my cabin, I shout for everyone to get the fuck out. Westcott is all who is left. And I give him a disappointed glare. He had one job, to keep Kai safe, and he couldn't do it.

Fuck him.

He's lucky if he has a job after I handle Milo.

I slam the door shut behind us, effectively locking out the entire world. And then I carry her to the door only she can unlock.

"Unlock it," I say.

She looks at me hesitantly, and I'm sure she can guess why I want to fuck her in her room. This is where I told her to go, and she defied me.

If she defies me now, she will regret it.

Slowly, she enters the password and shows her face, the key to unlocking her door.

I carry her inside the room that has never been slept in.

I throw her onto the bed.

"You promised me you would come here. You promised me you would be safe. Do you usually break your promises, Miss Miller?"

She breathes, heavily panting as her legs fall open on her bed. "I was safe."

I growl. "No, you weren't. The only place in the world you are safe is here."

She gives me a defiant look back. "You can't keep me trapped here forever."

"Oh, baby, you have no idea the lengths I will go to keep you safe."

"You promised you would set me free."

"And I will, when it's safe too."

"The world will never be safe."

I sigh. "It will be safer than it is right now."

"Promise me. Swear to me, you will let me go."

"When it's safe."

"No, when Milo is gone. When he is no longer a threat, you let me go free. Vow to me."

"I vow, when Milo is gone, you will be free."

We stare back at each other, neither of us relenting. Neither of us backing down from our threats and promises.

"And you promise me you will stay in this room until it's safe."

She doesn't answer me with words. She just shrugs off the shawl and unties her bikini top, knowing it will distract me from my goal.

"You'll stay here where you are safe from everybody, but me," I say as I remove my shirt over my head.

Her eyes soak me in, giving my body an appreciative stare. Most women appreciate my body, until they see the scars. The marks scare them. But not Kai, not when she understands the scars make me stronger, as they do her.

I slowly undo my belt and toss it on the bed next to her. She stares at it with wide seductive eyes. I don't usually bring toys into the bedroom, but tonight I need them. We both need to be punished for our actions.

Then I remove a condom from my pocket and toss it next to the belt. Only then do I remove my jeans and boxer briefs.

Kai looks at me with appreciation, like she's safe with me. She is anything but safe.

I attack. My body flying forward as I remove her shorts and bikini bottoms before my face plunges into her pussy. I'm relentless with my tongue. Building her too far, too fast, not caring enough to be merciful.

That's who we are. We are defiant and strong and push every button the other has.

And as much as I want her to follow my orders for once, it's why I care about her. It's why I'm so attracted to her. Because this is everything.

"God, Black! You're going to make me come in record time," she cries, her legs tightening around my ears.

I stop. She doesn't get to come. *Not yet.*

She moans at the loss of an orgasm.

I grab the belt in my hand. "Turn over."

She huffs, and her eyes gleam defiant. "You aren't using that on me."

I flip her over. "You deserve it after you broke your promise to me to stay safe." I pull her ass in the air and run the leather of my belt over her ass. The monster wants to beat her until her ass is so red she will never defy me again.

But the other part of me, the part I've only just discovered wants to whip her until her pussy is dripping in pleasure.

I don't know which part of me will win, and neither does she—that's what makes me so dangerous.

My cock hardens at the sight of her warm ass in the air. If my cock gets his way, I will pound into her ass and forget all about the whipping part.

"Enzo," Kai warns, as I run the belt over her perfect ass again. I know what her threat means. If I hurt her, she will do something to retaliate.

"You need to be punished," I say.

"No more than you. I'm not the only one who broke a promise."

"My vow to protect you overpowers any other promise. Every. Fucking. Time. I won't apologize for that."

Finally, she pushes her ass into the belt I have yet to use. "Then what are you waiting for?"

She knows exactly what I'm waiting for, the battle inside me to finish and winner to be crowned—either the monster or the protector. I don't know which will win.

But then her ass is pressing against my cock, and I don't have time to wait for the battle to finish.

I drop the belt, and my cock pushes against her ass.

"I guess my cock won," I say, hissing into her ear as I rub my cock against her sweet slickness between her legs.

"Enzo," she warns again, both concerned and thrilled by where my new thoughts are leading me.

"It's time I take another first. That seems like the proper punishment." And then I push my cock against her asshole. She clenches, not liking the intrusion.

"Relax, baby. Trust me."

My words are magic to her. Because even though I broke one promise, I kept the most important one. I kept her safe.

And I'm going to do better than that. I'm going to keep her safe forever.

I push harder as I kiss down her spine.

"Wow," she says, as I spread her open.

"I never imagined something could feel this tight," I groan as her ass cheeks clench around me.

I reach between her legs and find her most sensitive spot.

She relaxes immediately as I push all the way in.

"How does that feel so good?" she asks through a heavy breath.

"Because it's you and me, babe. We make everything better."

I pump into her as my fingers tease her clit, making her wetter and wetter. Her almost earlier orgasm is holding on, ready for a release.

"Why are you fucking me in the ass instead of my pussy? And why not before? This feels so incredible!" she cries.

"Because I wanted this to feel like a new beginning instead of a goodbye," I answer honestly.

We are both silent after that. Just feeling each other. Racing to make this moment last longer instead of shorter.

Hold out, don't come.

But of course, the moment ends as all the best moments do. With an explosion, new feelings stirring, and an empty feeling when it's all over.

I get dressed quickly, but she doesn't. She knows I won't let her out of this room again until Milo is dead.

When I'm finished dressing, I look at her almost reluctantly. I don't know what to do. *Tell her goodbye.* That I'm going to fight Milo. That I don't care if she hates me for holding her here. *She's safe.*

"Don't worry, I'm not going anywhere. You kept your promise; I'll be safe," Kai says.

But there is something haunting behind her words. Some truth she isn't speaking. She has her own secret. But then we always keep secrets from each other. It's one reason we would never work in a real relationship.

And I feel it. The moment our time is up. I'm losing her. And I can't keep holding onto her in this cage. She needs to be free. It's time for me to slay the dragon to save the princess. But this isn't a fairytale. Once, I defeat the dragon, I won't be walking away with the princess.

And so I walk out without a goodbye or a promise. I walk away, hoping I can free her. And hoping her secret won't destroy her. I walk away without a goodbye, even though I know it is one.

26

KAI

Enzo leaves me naked and alone.

He leaves without a proper goodbye. Although, after what he did to my body, it felt like a goodbye.

It felt like death.

Enzo left me to keep his promise to me—the promise that no man will ever hurt me.

But he doesn't know I made my own secret promise. I would never let him risk his life to save mine.

I couldn't let him die saving me.

Enzo won't understand. He thinks after how royally he fucked up that it's his responsibility to protect me.

But I'm the one who is in love with him. He doesn't love me. He will get over my absence. He will be able to move on with his life—eventually.

But if Enzo were to die, I wouldn't live. My love is too much. And his death would end us both.

So I did the only thing I could to ensure one of us survived. To ensure Enzo survives long enough to keep the Black empire thriving. To bear an heir. To continue the legacy.

I didn't betray Enzo before, and I didn't now. But to Enzo, what I did will feel like the biggest betrayal of all.

But waiting now is the worst part. Now I have to put my trust in other people to keep Enzo safe. I know they will because they want what I have to offer. And I will do anything to keep Enzo safe.

Slowly, I get up and get dressed, putting my bikini and shorts back on as time moves too slowly.

I pace around the room, not really taking any of it in.

This isn't my room, it never was, and never will be. It's just a cage Enzo created to keep me locked in.

I try to focus on anything else, the gentle rocking of the boat, the humming of the air conditioning, or the warmth of the sun through the window. But it's useless.

All I can feel is him.

He's everywhere.

Inside me.

Around me.

Engulfing me in everything he is. And I want to revel in every drop of him. Because the beauty encompassing Enzo squashes all of the darkness.

But that beautiful floating feeling changes quickly.

I can't describe the feeling.

But my gut clenches.

My heart stops.

My world ends.

Something happened.

Something is wrong.

No!

I run to the door and to my surprise, the door opens. I assumed Enzo had locked it from the outside, but there is no need for him to lock it when he left a guard to watch over me—Zeke.

"What's wrong?" he asks.

I hold my stomach, feeling something in the depths of my core. I've never felt this way before. It's like a stirring of danger.

I glance at Liesel, who is leaning against the door in the hallway behind Zeke. Everyone Enzo left must have been ordered into the cabins behind the safety of the security system. I was to stay behind one more level of security in my bedroom.

The feeling is what Liesel described earlier—knowing that danger is coming.

"Danger. Enzo is in danger," I say feeling it so intensely that I can practically feel the pain myself.

Zeke looks into me trying to understand how I could be feeling this. "You're sure?"

"Yes."

"Fuck!" he curses, letting me go, obviously torn between going to Enzo's rescue and staying here and protecting me.

"We need to go," I say.

"No, Enzo's orders were clear. I keep you here where it's safe."

I smile softly, "Since when do we follow Enzo's orders?"

Liesel frowns from behind Zeke. "You promised to protect Enzo. You swore to me."

"This is me keeping that promise," I say.

I look up at Zeke. "What do you say? Are we going to save the world or what? At least our little piece of it?"

"Not until you put something a little more protective on you," he says.

I hide my smile as I run back into my room, throw on some jeans and a sweatshirt and return.

Zeke hands me a gun, which I take and tuck into my

jeans like I've seen all the men do. My hair falls into my face as I do.

He pulls the scrunchie tying his own hair back and hands it to me. "Tie your hair back. I don't want the reason you miss shooting Milo is because your hair was in your face."

I raise an eyebrow as I smile and tie my hair back out of my face. "What about you?"

"I have perfect aim whether my hair is in my face or not. Let's go," he says.

Liesel stands in my way as we try to leave. "Don't hurt him."

"I won't. I love him."

"Then live long enough for him to learn to love you back," Liesel says before walking away, letting Zeke and I go.

The pit in my stomach doesn't leave; in fact, it intensifies as we get on the smaller boat and speed off into the night. I don't know if I'm making the right move or just putting Enzo into greater danger. But I can't just stay behind. I have to try, even if I die.

27

ENZO

I STAND on the stern of my boat, watching Milo's yacht face my fleet. Rowan's yacht is to my left. But this isn't going to be a battle of yachts; this is a battle of men.

Rowan may pretend to be on my side, but I know he's not. Langston confirmed the truth. Rowan has a vendetta against my father. He may not truly be on Milo's side either, but the two enemies may form together to take down a worse enemy. And I'm that worse enemy. I'm the worst it gets.

Because I have nothing to lose. And I fight like death means nothing to me. And I'll face my father's crimes, even though I didn't commit them.

They think I have something to lose—Kai.

But I can't lose her, not when she's locked away in the safest place possible.

And dying isn't a curse; it's a blessing. So I will fight as fearless as I always do.

"You ready to surrender?" I shout to Milo.

He laughs. "Are you? I think we have you outnumbered."

"We? It looks like just you," I say, putting my foot up on the railing like I'm going to a cruise instead of about to launch myself over the railing onto his yacht. I pretend I don't already know the truth, that Rowan is on his side.

Milo's eyes cut, and I know that's his cue.

But I'm faster.

I shoot Rowan before he has a chance to make a move on me. I watch his lifeless body drop to the floor.

Seconds later, my men have Rowan's entire crew surrendering.

"Now, as I was saying. Would you like to surrender?" I ask. "It seems you are a bit outnumbered."

Milo frowns. "I don't surrender to men who can't keep their word."

"I kept my word. Your quarrel was with Rowan. He's dead now. Now you deal with me."

Bullets fire, and we attack.

The rest goes by in a blur.

The orders I give.

The gunfire.

The screams of pain.

The bloodshed.

All of it moves so slowly and so quickly. Until all that I'm left with is me and Milo. Everything disappears into the background.

"You hurt her," I say.

"I did. And I will again," Milo answers.

"Over my dead body."

"That's the plan."

Our guns are pointed in each other's direction, but I feel her before I see her—Kai. *What the hell is she doing here?*

And then I hear the crack of the gun, and I know I've lost her.

"Kai!" I yell, begging for the bullet to miss. To not hit her. To go anywhere but her.

Zeke is standing next to her, I spot Langston holding is own wound on his side, but he will never make it to her in time. But Zeke can and does.

He dives in front of her and pushes her to the ground. The bullet hits him square in the heart.

I knew I loved Zeke, but not until this moment of watching him die, saving my woman did I realize how much. I thought my heart was a cage of metal and stone, only there to hold my monster inside, but it's a heart all the same. A heart capable of breaking, shattering, and ripping in half. And that's what I feel. *All of it.*

No amount of pain my body could experience is greater than losing someone I love. I learned that with my mother, but I thought it was because I was a kid. I was young, but now I know it wasn't because I was a kid. It's because this is what love does; it is everything when you have it and then takes everything away when it's gone and leaves nothing but the dull pain behind.

I don't have time to go through all the stages of grief in a single moment, but that's what my body tries to do. I feel denial, reality, bargaining, pain, all of it. *And I hate it.*

Kai sobs over Zeke's lifeless body.

She's alive, and I made a vow to protect her—no matter what. No matter how she fucked up. It's time to make good on that promise.

All of my anger, rage, and pain take over, and I charge at Milo. This won't be won with guns. He made this personal, and I'm going to kill him with my bare hands.

My fist connects with his face, bloodying his nose, and making contact with his eyes.

He stumbles backward, but I don't relent. I attack ruthlessly over and over. My fists flying, my legs kicking. He tries to fight back, but it's clear he's not used to fighting hand to hand with someone his own size. So instead, he moves to a defensive stance. His body blocking blow after blow. It will take longer for me to kill him this way, but I don't care. *I have time.*

But the world is never on my side.

A storm is coming, and I don't mean just my fists. The ship begins rocking at an unsafe level as rains pour down upon us.

This needs to end—now.

"This is for Zeke," I scream, putting everything into my attack, my entire body drives into Milo's. I don't care about the consequences of my attack on myself; I just want this motherfucker dead.

My force is too much for either of us, as our bodies collide, we hit the railing that breaks, and then we fall down to the ocean depths.

Our bodies stay connected as we hit the water, and now we both rely on the other for survival. The only way we live is if we both live. If we both surface. But I'd rather us both die, than Milo live.

So I force our bodies lower under the water. Milo fights against my hold on his neck and body, keeping him down. But my hold is tighter. Our oxygen levels deplete more and more with every second that passes. It will happen soon. Death is coming, and it will be sweet.

I look up and see light. *This is it—the end.*

A light descends further upon us.

Wait, it doesn't make sense. In death, I shouldn't be headed for a light. I should be headed to the darkness of hell.

But that doesn't stop the light from grabbing me. I let go

of Milo and watch his body float down, away from me as the light takes me up.

I hit the surface of the water and take a deep breath, my lungs heaving for oxygen but not getting enough. I vomit up the salt water before I can finally take a breath.

"Thank fuck, you're alive," Kai cries, holding me to her.

She saved me.

I look behind me, but I don't see Milo surface.

She kisses me hard as the rain pours down on us, and I know as much as I want to spend my life making out with her here, I can't. *It's not safe.*

"We have to go," I say.

She nods, and we swim for the ladder on the yacht. When we reach the deck, Langston finds us, gripping his side where a bullet grazed him.

"The men have the yacht ready to go. We need to leave," Langston says.

I nod. "Where is Zeke?" I ask. *I need his body. I need to bury him properly.*

"He's gone. Went overboard in the storm," Langston adds.

"Let's go," I say, even though I want to dive back into the ocean and pull Zeke's body from the depths myself.

We all board the boat that will take us back to our yacht and stand on the edge, looking out into the dark ocean. The moon and stars twinkle overhead as we mourn a man we all loved.

Langston loved Zeke as a brother.

I loved Zeke as a friend.

And Kai loved Zeke as her protector.

"He deserved better than to be shot by a man like Milo," I say, refusing to cry as I lean over the railing looking down into the water.

"He would have been honored to die protecting someone he loves," Langston says, and a tear drips from each of our eyes.

"And he'll rest in the sea he loved," Kai finishes. She removes the scrunchie from her hair and places it on her wrist. A scrunchie I recognize as Zeke's.

His hair wasn't always long. He'd go through periods of it being long and short. But when it was long, he always carried a scrunchie for when his hair got in the way. We used to make fun of him, calling him a girl. Now I want him back just so I can tease his giant ass. I want him back so he can tease me back. So he can tell me how stupid I'm being. I want him by my side when we fight, when we drink, when we sail. But he won't be, ever again.

Kai kisses the scrunchie. "We will miss you big guy. You have no idea how much you were loved."

I meet her eyes; you have no idea how much you are loved, stingray.

28

ENZO

WE SAILED BACK TO MIAMI.

There is no reason to keep running on the ocean now that Milo is gone. All that is left is to keep my promise to Kai to set her free.

Kai has used her own room since we got back on the yacht. She hasn't been in my bed since before I went after Milo. At first, I thought it was because we were all mourning Zeke's death and needed our space, but then I realized the truth, she's distancing herself from me to make the next step easier.

We made port in Miami yesterday. There is nothing keeping her here anymore, except the truth.

The truth could keep her here, trapped forever. But I realized something the second that Zeke died. I realized just how capable of love I am. *And I love Kai Miller.*

I love her more than I could ever love Zeke or Langston. The love is different. It's all consuming, unhealthy in some ways, and like breathing air in other ways. My love for Kai is greater than anything I've ever felt before. It's greater than the pain my father made me endure.

It's greater than losing my mother.

It's greater than losing Zeke.

Losing Kai would top everything I've ever felt. But I can't keep her trapped here any longer. If I love her, she deserves to be free. She deserves the chance to choose her own life and future. I won't take that from her any longer. Even to keep her safe. There are other ways to protect her.

I take out my phone and scroll to Kai's contact. I change it until it reads, My Love. And then I text her.

ME: Meet me in the lounge.

MY LOVE: Five minutes.

THOSE FIVE MINUTES are the longest of my life. Because I know what I'm about to do, and I don't know what the outcome will be. But I have to do it; if I truly love Kai, I have to set her free.

She looks like a goddess in an all white bikini cover-up, her jet black hair cascading down her back in thick strands, and Zeke's scrunchie on her wrist—I doubt she will ever take the scrunchie off.

"One last game of truth or lies?" I ask, pouring a couple of shots of the disgusting alcohol she poured us before.

"Last?" she asks, stepping into the room.

I nod.

"Okay," she says, looking concerned as she takes the shot glass from me. This time we don't make ourselves comfortable on the couch, there will be nothing comfortable about this. This will be the most uncomfortable, painful thing I've done.

"I promised to protect you forever, truth or lie?" I ask.

"Truth," she says, not taking the shot, just holding it in her hands.

"And have I kept that promise?"

"Yes."

"I promised to set you free when Milo is gone, truth or lie?"

"Truth."

"Milo is dead, truth or lie?"

"Truth," Kai says, swallowing hard.

I hold my shot up, as does she, and then we both drink it, because we both know what is coming next. The drink burns going down, but it doesn't hurt as much as what will come next.

I won't tell her I love her. It's not fair to her if I do. If I tell her I love her, that might make her decision for her. And that's not what freedom is about. Freedom is about giving a person a chance to choose, and that's what I'm doing.

"You are free, truth or lie?" I ask, my voice breathy.

"Truth," she breathes back.

I nod.

"Thank you," she whispers.

Stay. I love you. Stay. We will figure out everything else. I will keep you safe. Just stay.

"I should go," she says.

I nod. *I can't form words.*

She opens her mouth like she wants to speak but then closes it.

"You aren't going to try to protect me anymore, right? That's what being free is," Kai says.

I clear my throat. "I won't protect you anymore," I lie.

"Thank you."

"And you won't protect me," I say.

"I won't protect you," she lies.

And then she's gone.

I follow up to the top deck to watch her leave. Langston joins me.

"Why are you letting her go when you know Milo is still out there? You know he survived," Langston says.

"Because it's the only way to save her."

"What? That makes no sense."

"It doesn't, but it's the truth." Unlike everything we just said to each other. Everything we said before was lies. I will always try to protect her. And she will always try to protect me.

We both knew Milo is still alive.

We both knew the other tried to make a deal with the devil himself.

But Milo will only take one of our deals—mine. He will not take Kai. Kai will be free. And when the deal is done, Kai will disappear into the crowd. She will no longer be in danger. She will get a fresh start.

She will be safe; I'll make Langston swear to that.

She will always be protected; even if she never learns of the love I have for her, she will be safe. That's the promise I vowed to keep no matter what. No matter if I have to sacrifice my own life to keep it.

29

KAI

Kai's Lie

ENZO GAVE ME MY FREEDOM.

Or at least the illusion of freedom.

He set me free. He gave me the one thing I've been asking for since he took me.

I should be happy, grateful, elated.

Instead, I'm focused on saving Enzo from the danger.

I'm tired of fighting.

I'm tired of losing people. Zeke is enough. I can't bear to lose Enzo too.

So I lied to Enzo.

Repeatedly.

I lied when I said Milo was dead, when I overheard Enzo and Langston talking about Milo being alive.

I lied when I said I wouldn't protect Enzo, because the only thing I care about is keeping him safe.

And I lied to myself when I pretended I can survive being separated from Enzo—I can't.

I made a deal with the devil to keep Enzo safe.

When Milo came to the yacht searching for me before the war started, we had a moment to talk—alone.

And I gave him what he wanted—me.

I would give myself to Milo freely and willingly for the rest of my life, if he sparred Enzo. If he let Enzo live, then I would be his. If he let the Black empire remain Enzo's, I would be his.

Milo said he would consider my offer and left. I yelled into the darkness if he killed Enzo, even if Enzo provoked him first, the deal was off. I would never be his.

And I could see in Milo's eyes as he drove off into the night how badly he wanted me. He wanted me more than he wanted the empire. That's who Milo is. Women he keeps as slaves are his ultimate goal. Not money, and not power over men. Power over women—that's what he wants. *And I'm his ultimate prize.*

I know Enzo tried to make his own deal with Milo. But I know Milo will take my deal, because he loves controlling women more than he loves money and power.

I will save you Enzo. I will save you from any more pain or loss. You've already lost too much. I will keep you from losing more.

I find the number Milo gave me to contact him when I'm ready to make the deal. And then I dial.

30

ENZO

Enzo's Lie

"Where are you going?" Langston asks.

"To make a phone call," I say, walking back into my private cabins. I don't need Langston following me and trying to stop me.

The guilt eats at me as I walk. *Is it okay to lie to those you love, even to protect them?*

I'm sure it's a sin, but one I'm willing to commit again and again to keep Kai safe.

Because the lies I told her were limitless.

I claimed Milo was dead when we both knew he wasn't.

I lied when I said I wouldn't protect her—I always will.

And I lied when I didn't tell her I loved her.

I should have told her. Maybe that would have changed everything. Or maybe it would have risked everything. Because the only way to keep her safe is to make this deal. She deserves a life free of all of this.

Away from Milo.

Away from Black.

Away from me.

I made a deal that ensures she will be free and protected forever.

As soon as I realized Milo was alive, I lost it. I wanted him dead. But we watched him. After news of Rowan's death spread, my enemies all converged and sided with Milo. They will all attack together because they see the Black empire as too big, too powerful. I'm too big of a threat. And it would be suicide to fight them all at the same time.

The only way to end Milo and keep Kai safe is to give everything to Milo.

So when I realized Milo was alive, I made a phone call. I offered up everything he has ever wanted. I named him my heir. Found some deep buried blood connection and said if I were to die, he could fight in my place to become Black.

When the games start, Langston will make sure Kai never shows up to fight. Milo will win by default. He will become Black. He will get my entire life's work. He will get what my father and generations of Millers and Rinaldis before fought so hard to build.

He will get to kill me and claim the Black empire. He will get everything he's ever wanted.

I know Kai made her own deal with Milo. But he won't take it. She offered him her body, while I'm offering him a chance to kill me and take an entire empire.

Milo will choose my deal. Kai will be safe.

I find Milo's contact and dial the number. I will sacrifice everything to save her.

31

MILO

I sit on my throne in my home in Italy, triumphant.

I won.

Enzo Black thought he did when we hit the water. He had no idea days later he would surrender everything to me.

He had no idea the woman he loves had already surrendered herself to me before the war even started.

I had won before the battle begun.

Enzo needed his woman to save him in the water that day, but I grew up in the sea. I know how to fight, hold my breath, and swim for the surface.

I know how to survive. And that's what I did until my men found me.

And now, I have all the power.

Because I get to choose which life I take. I get to choose between the two fools.

Both Enzo and Kai are willing to give up everything to save the other—for true love.

Ugh, it makes me sick.

I can't believe either was foolish enough to fall in love.

Love is a weakness. It makes you vulnerable. Case in point, both of them are willing to give up their lives in order to save the other.

And it makes getting to choose who I take all the sweeter.

Both are strong.

Both are fighters.

Both are stupid enough to fall in love.

Both hold the key to me taking over the Black empire.

But I have to make a choice.

I can't pick both, as tempting as it is. If I kill both, then I won't get to watch as the other crumbles into a pile of dust —self-destructing from the loss of the other.

Both think they are doing the right thing by saving the other. But neither realize by sacrificing themselves they are killing the one they leave behind. *That is how love works.*

So I must choose. And I know exactly who I will pick. I will pick the strongest. The one most likely to become Black. The one who will fight until they become Black and earn me an empire. And then I will make them sacrifice their life, love, and empire to me.

The End

Thank you so much for reading! Kai and Enzo's story continues in Stolen by Truths!

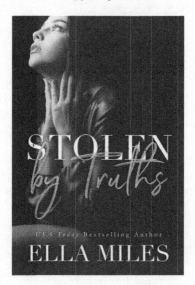

FREE BOOKS

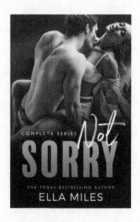

Read **Not Sorry** for **FREE**! And sign up to get my latest releases, updates, and more goodies here→<u>EllaMiles.com/freebooks</u>

Follow me on BookBub to get notified of my new releases and recommendations here→Follow on BookBub Here

Join Ella's Bellas FB group for giveaways and FUN & a
FREE copy of **Pretend I'm Yours**→Join Ella's Bellas Here

ALSO BY ELLA MILES

TRUTH OR LIES (Coming 2019):

Lured by Lies #0.5

Taken by Lies #1

Betrayed by Truths #2

Trapped by Lies #3

Stolen by Truths #4

Possessed by Lies #5

Consumed by Truths #6

DIRTY SERIES:

Dirty Beginning

Dirty Obsession

Dirty Addiction

Dirty Revenge

Dirty: The Complete Series

ALIGNED SERIES:

Aligned: Volume 1 (Free Series Starter)

Aligned: Volume 2

Aligned: Volume 3

Aligned: Volume 4

Aligned: The Complete Series Boxset

UNFORGIVABLE SERIES:

Heart of a Thief

Heart of a Liar

Heart of a Prick

Unforgivable: The Complete Series Boxset

MAYBE, DEFINITELY SERIES:

Maybe Yes

Maybe Never

Maybe Always

Definitely Yes

Definitely No

Definitely Forever

STANDALONES:

Pretend I'm Yours

Finding Perfect

Savage Love

Too Much

Not Sorry

ABOUT THE AUTHOR

Ella Miles writes steamy romance, including everything from dark suspense romance that will leave you on the edge of your seat to contemporary romance that will leave you laughing out loud or crying. Most importantly, she wants you to feel everything her characters feel as you read.

Ella is currently living her own happily ever after near the Rocky Mountains with her high school sweetheart husband. Her heart is also taken by her goofy five year old black lab who is scared of everything, including her own shadow.

Ella is a USA Today Bestselling Author & Top 50 Bestselling Author.

Stalk Ella at:
www.ellamiles.com
ella@ellamiles.com